LAURA TAYLOR
Wildflower

Silhouette Desire

Published by Silhouette Books New York

America's Publisher of Contemporary Romance

SILHOUETTE BOOKS
300 East 42nd St., New York, N.Y. 10017

ISBN: 0-373-05501-3

First Silhouette Books printing June 1989

Printed in the U.S.A.

"Say Something, Alexa!"

Gray stopped his pacing and towered over her.

"There isn't anything to say, other than the obvious," she told him.

"Which is?" he demanded.

"I won't have an affair with you."

Anger tightened Gray's jaw and brought winter ice into his dark eyes. "How sensible and mature," he snapped.

"Can't you just accept the fact that we both got carried away?"

"No, because it would be a lie. There's a lot more going on here, Alexa, so don't try and run away from me. There isn't anyplace to go."

Alexa flared defensively. "Don't you dare threaten me, Grayson Lennox, you have no right."

"Then don't lie to me or to yourself. I felt your hunger when you were in my arms, and I've had a taste of all that passion you've got locked up inside you. It's mine, Alexa, every ounce of it. I want it *and* you, and I'll have both."

Dear Reader:

I hope you've been enjoying 1989, our "Year of the Man" at Silhouette Desire. Every one of the twelve authors who are contributing a *Man of the Month* has created a very special someone for your reading pleasure. Each man is unique, and each author's style and characterization give you a different insight into her man's story.

From January to December, 1989 will be a twelve-month extravaganza spotlighting one book each month with special cover treatment as a tribute to the Silhouette Desire hero—our *Man of the Month*!

Created by your favorite authors, these men are utterly captivating—and I think Mr. June, Annette Broadrick's Quinn McNamara, will be simply...*Irresistible*! One of Lass Small's Lambert sisters gets a very special man in July. *Man of the Month* Graham Rawlins may start as the *Odd Man Out*, but that doesn't last long....

Yours,

Isabel Swift

Senior Editor & Editorial Coordinator

Books by Laura Taylor

Silhouette Desire

Troubled Waters #407
Wildflower #501

LAURA TAYLOR

views life as a potpourri of drama, fantasy and humor. Dedicated to writing both romance and mainstream novels, she feels strongly about her dual professional commitments. With a degree in criminology and a background as an Air Force brat and the wife of a former Marine Corps aviator—her "real-life" *Top Gun* hero—and a passion for travel and adventure, she now divides her time between her home in the southern Ozarks of Arkansas and visits with her family in California.

One

My husband hates me, and I've grown to hate myself in the months since our marriage. Lying to him was wrong, but I was afraid...afraid to face my parents, and the world, without a father for my child.

We were friends once, but that's in the past. He'll never trust me again. He's said as much, and I believe him. I'm paying for my mistake, though. I'm trapped in a marriage built on lies.

I often ask myself why I didn't have the courage to call off the wedding before it was too late. Alexa has already begun to pay for my foolishness, even though she's only an infant. Seeing her as a symbol of my deceit, Jack has grown hard and distant. He won't ever let me forget that I came into our marriage carrying another man's child.

God, please forgive me, because I haven't found a way to forgive myself. I shouldn't have married him...it was for

*all the wrong reasons, even though I believed I was doing the
right thing at the time.*

Alexa Rivers struggled to fight the panic churning inside
her as she stood before the wall mirror in the dressing room
reserved for the young women of her wedding party. Like
the relentless waves of a storm's assault on an undefended
beach, her mother's words continued to hammer at her.

*I shouldn't have married him. I shouldn't have married
him.*

She raised shaking hands and pressed her fingertips to her
temples, suddenly aware that she was about to make the
biggest mistake of her life if she married Tom Henderson.
Her mother had married in haste and panic, and she'd lived
to regret her decision.

Calm and collected until a few short hours ago, Alexa
now felt a bone-deep chill and a sense of isolation unlike
anything she'd ever experienced, despite the warmth of the
California June morning and thanks to the diary she'd discovered in a box of her mother's long-stored treasures.

She'd just wanted to complete the bridal tradition of the
something old that would complement the something new
and the something blue she'd already received at her bridal
shower. A small memento of her mother, the one source of
love and comfort she'd depended upon until her untimely
death when Alexa was twelve. Instead, she'd unearthed her
mother's despair and heartache, not to mention the startling truth of her own parentage.

She couldn't go through with this wedding. She couldn't
marry a man she wasn't in love with and ruin both their
lives.

*I shouldn't have married him. I shouldn't have married
him.*

The haunting refrain echoed in her mind and pummeled
her senses, further heightening already disarrayed emo-

tions. Deaf to the comments of her girlfriends and oblivious to the chatter and laughter bouncing off the old whitewashed adobe walls of the landmark Santa Barbara church, Alexa abruptly turned away from the mirror and walked out of the dressing room.

As if by prearrangement, she spotted Tom standing in the hallway. She hurried toward him, her pace urgent and her facial features ashen.

"Oh, Tom, I'm sorry, but I can't go through with it," she burst out. "I can't marry you. It's wrong, and we both know it."

She suddenly ran short of words and stared at him, trembling with a brand of panic totally foreign to her. She wanted to run into his arms and beg his forgiveness. He was her friend, the best friend she'd ever had, and now she was hurting him.

"Calm down, Alexa. You're just having a last-minute case of wedding jitters. Everything's going to be fine, you'll see."

His tone was so typically Tommy that she almost laughed. She longed to laugh, but she didn't dare because what was building inside her was edging closer and closer to hysteria.

He grasped her hands and drew her into a shallow alcove just off the hallway. Despite his surprise at Alexa's uncharacteristic lack of composure, Tom's appreciative gaze drifted down her willowy, lace-covered figure before returning to the finely sculpted contours of her pale face and the distress blazing in her large blue-gray eyes.

She shook her head to clear her muddled brain. The awkward gesture lacked the grace normally so innate to her every move. "Tommy, you're not listening. We can't do this. *I* can't do it. I thought I could, I even wanted to, but I just can't."

She fought the rush of emotion that made her eyes sting and threatened to close her throat. *He doesn't deserve this. Neither one of us deserves this.*

"You know how much I care about you, but we can't get married, not even for Jack."

Jack Rivers: mastermind of the wedding of the year; entrepreneurial genius; favorite son of the state of California; empire builder; philanthropist; supreme manipulator of people and events; Tom Henderson's employer; and her father—no, not her real father, she realized once again, still reeling from the contents of her mother's diary.

"Then what *do* you want?"

Shock and an odd sense of relief mingled inside her as she considered his question. The tears she'd been fighting thwarted her and spilled from her eyes. Tom frowned before handing her a swatch of white linen. He waited patiently while she blotted her cheeks and dried her eyes.

"Talk to me, Alexa," he urged. "Tell me what's going on."

"I can't. Forgive me, but I just can't talk about any of it yet." Clutching the now damp handkerchief, she whispered raggedly, "Tom, listen to me, please. We don't love each other and friendship isn't enough. We'd only end up hating one another..." *Like my parents.* Knowing now why her parents had loathed one another hurt even more than the cold war she'd endured as a child. "I was a fool to let things go this far."

Voices rose in the hallway, as if to further indict her poor judgment. A florist hurried by the open door, briefly catching their attention as she helped an assistant carry a last-minute addition to the collection of large pink and white rose-filled crystal vases scattered throughout the church.

The strains of organ music filled the air. She realized that their guests had already begun to arrive. She knew, too, that her father would personally greet each and every one of them—all four hundred of them. That was his style. And no one had ever been able to change Jack Rivers, least of all his daughter.

"Where are your things?"

Alexa stared at him, bewildered by his abrupt question until she realized that he was talking about the trousseau she'd assembled for their three-week honeymoon in the Caribbean. "Still in my car, but why?"

"What's your cash situation?" Loyal friend and perennially practical accountant, Tom's dual personas, merged.

"Traveler's checks, much more than I need. A gift from Jack." Money. Her father's apparent solution for everything.

"How much time do you want?"

Alexa welcomed his orderly questions because they put a temporary cap on the anxiety threatening to submerge her. "I'm not sure. A few weeks, maybe longer."

"If you go now, you'll have to come back one hundred and fifty percent in charge of your life. You can't mess around if you don't want Jack taking over again. Otherwise, leaving will simply amount to grandstanding."

She knew he was right. It was one of the few coherent thoughts she'd managed all morning. Alexa lifted her hand and shakily smoothed back the strawberry blond tendrils of hair that had already begun to escape the intricate topknot her hairdresser had arranged. "I'm sorry, Tommy, please believe me."

He took her by the shoulders, ever the protective friend. "I didn't walk into this with my eyes closed, Alexa. I also thought it was what you wanted. I would never have gone along with the idea of a wedding if I hadn't truly believed that. You already know I think passion's pretty overrated as the basis for a marriage," he said, referring to his first failed marriage.

He smiled wistfully. "Friendship just seemed easier, a sounder foundation for a long-term relationship. Look, you're sensitive, caring and pretty terrific to look at. What man in his right mind would say no to a combination like that?"

She simply looked at him, the bleakness of her expression telling him what her voice couldn't express.

"Alexa, it's not the end of the world because you've decided to change your mind, so have a clear conscience where I'm concerned, okay?"

"Just promise you won't hate me for running out on you this way."

"Stop with the dramatics!" he said affectionately. "Everything will turn out fine."

Still troubled by the possible repercussions of her actions, Alexa knew she couldn't let him cajole her into thinking that she was without responsibility for the chaos she was about to set into motion.

"What if Jack fires you?" Alexa asked tensely, her eyes wide with renewed anxiety. She knew her father well, too well. "He's liable to, you know. He hates it when things don't turn out the way he plans them."

Tom grinned almost boyishly as he tugged her into his arms for a quick hug. "So he fires me. I'm thirty-two years old and I've always wanted to open my own consulting business. You aren't the only one who needs to make some changes for the better. I think it's about time we *both* took some risks."

She stepped back, wonder in her eyes as she considered the good fortune of knowing this man. "Tommy, you amaze me some of the time."

His expression very nearly placid, he looked down at her. "You're my best friend, Alexa, so be happy. I'll cover for you as best I can with Jack, but eventually you'll have to see him and have it out with him. You owe it to yourself. And to him," he added as a judicious afterthought.

"I don't know what to say to you."

"Then don't say anything. Just do what you have to do, Alexa, and call me in a day or two so I'll know you're all right. That way nobody'll worry, especially Jack."

She seriously doubted the worried part of Tom's comment, but she didn't say anything.

Tom's expression grew thoughtful. "You know, for a while I thought our getting married was the right answer for both of us. It's the only reason I ever even agreed to it. I'm tired of living alone, and I know how much having a family means to you."

She indulged herself for a moment and studied him, her fingertips resting on the sleeve of his white tuxedo as they faced one another. She knew him well enough to realize that his pale green eyes hid his sense of humor, his thinning auburn hair topped an athletic body, and his gentle disposition would be a special gift to the children she hoped he would one day father.

Her feelings shone in her eyes. "Thank you, Tom."

He smiled indulgently before glancing at his watch. "We don't have much time."

"I still don't like the idea of you facing my father alone," she persisted, still worried.

He tugged at the bow tie fastened at his throat and unbuttoned the collar of his white dress shirt. "He's just a man, Alexa, and we all put our pants on the same way."

She laughed, the giddy sound a reflection of the current state of her nerves. "You can really handle standing in front of a church packed to the rafters and admit your prospective bride took a quick hike out of town?"

He nodded, although he looked faintly awed at the prospect of the job. "Piece o' cake," he quipped with a snap of his fingers.

She suddenly understood his strange mood. "You're relieved, aren't you?"

He shifted awkwardly. "The truth?"

"The *whole* truth, Tom."

"Very relieved. I don't want to make another mistake,
either," he said quietly. "You'll have to slip out the back
door at the end of the hall and take your car. Where's your
purse?"

Alexa glanced at the door of the room she had just va-
cated.

"Wait here, I'll get it for you."

"But I need to change," she stage-whispered as loudly as
she dared while gesturing at the French lace covering her
from throat to toes.

"No time, sweets," he said, already across the hall. "It'd
be like waving a red flag at a bull. And don't stop at the
house. There'll be too many servants around."

"But—"

He pressed his index finger to his lips. Alexa didn't say
another word. Tom rapped lightly on the door, eased it open
and disappeared inside.

As she waited for him Alexa thought about her home, the
two-bedroom gate house situated at the edge of her father's
estate in the hills overlooking Santa Barbara. It was the one
place where she could really relax when she wasn't serving
as her father's official hostess or working at Rivers House.

Just the thought of walking away, even for two or three
weeks, from the children of Rivers House made her heart
ache. She would miss them, but she knew that the counsel-
ors there were the best in the country. The trust fund her
mother had left for the orphanage guaranteed it. Alexa
further insured it by personally administering the trust herself, despite her father's constant harping that any fool
could be hired to do the job.

Tom returned quickly. Handing her the white leather shoulder bag, he hustled her down the now deserted corridor. "Call me once you get wherever it is you're headed."

Alexa saw by the look on his face that he didn't want to know her exact plans. She was glad, because she only had a vague idea of her destination herself. And she certainly didn't want Tom to lie for her. He was doing more than enough by giving her gifts of friendship and understanding.

Alexa found that concentrating on the heavy weekend summer traffic had several benefits. Driving temporarily prevented her from dwelling on the disastrous events of the morning. It also helped settle her frayed nerves. As the hours unfolded and traffic thinned, she headed east and then north into central California.

Alexa soon realized that she'd behaved immaturely by abandoning Tom to the questionable mercy of her father and their wedding guests. Bolting like a nervous filly at the starting gate of a high-stakes race had never been her style.

She had always prided herself on her reputation as a rational and thoughtful person, as well as someone who had a pronounced reluctance to express herself in emotional extremes. Friends viewed her as dependable and considerate. Her father's business cronies considered her decorative, conversant about current affairs and amenable to the wishes of her manipulative parent.

Until today, she realized with a vague sense of pride. Today, she was certain that she'd shocked them all.

Calm and determination slowly replaced the panic that had upended her senses and thrown her emotions off balance. Alexa decided that her decision to leave, to give herself time to think, had been the right one, despite the incipient hysteria of those final moments in the church and the unorthodox nature of her departure.

Intent on putting as many miles as possible between herself and Santa Barbara, Alexa stopped twice for gas, silently endured the curious stares of several gas station attendants and continued north. She used the facilities of a deserted roadside rest stop, grateful for both the privacy and the opportunity to stretch her cramped legs.

Aware that her appearance in a restaurant would prompt curious questions, she decided to delay eating until she could enlist the aid of an understanding female willing to help her out of a fitted wedding gown that buttoned from nape to waist and wrists to elbows. A maid at a motel made the most sense, but first she had to find suitable lodging before she could stop for the night.

As she made her way along the twisting two-lane road east of Stockton, Alexa sighed heavily and rubbed the back of her neck. Both the sound and the gesture reflected not only her still somewhat vandalized emotions, but also her uncertainty about the future and the fatigue of traveling three hundred miles since midmorning.

Dusk crept across the rolling hills on either side of the narrow road with its usual stealth. Alexa, mulling over the best way to solve the mess she'd just managed to make of her life, absently reached out and flipped a dashboard switch to turn on the car's headlights.

Glancing quickly at her map, she estimated that it wouldn't be long before she reached the town of Jackson. Following a late dinner and a good night's sleep, she planned to complete the drive south to Lake Tahoe the next morning. Hopefully, a former college girlfriend would be willing to house her for a night or two until she could make other plans.

Something small and furry unexpectedly darted across the road several yards ahead of her car. Startled by the sudden appearance of an animal on the otherwise deserted stretch of pavement, Alexa sucked in a quick breath and slammed her foot on the brake pedal. She was even less prepared for the small boy who hurled himself onto the road in pursuit of the four-legged creature. Oblivious to the risks to herself, Alexa instinctively wrenched the steering wheel hard to the right.

She struggled to regain control of her car as it veered onto the rutted shoulder of the road. Bouncing and skidding at an odd angle across the uneven stretch of dirt and rocks, the vehicle took brief flight over a shallow culvert, crashed through a section of fence line and finally came to a halt in the unyielding embrace of a wide-trunked oak.

Sprawled across the steering wheel, Alexa drifted in and out of shock. She didn't see the stricken expression on the face of the boy who had unwittingly caused her accident, nor was she aware of his mounting terror when he saw the blood dripping from the gash on her chin.

Several minutes ticked by. Smoke and steam erupted from the overheated engine of her car and shifted upward into the night air. Clinging to consciousness by the sheer force of her will, she lifted her head. Pain throbbed in her temple. The ache in her left shoulder suggested that she'd struck the steering wheel with tremendous force. As she tried to take stock of her situation, she noted that the doors of her car had popped open on impact.

The engine continued to pop and hiss, cautioning a still dazed Alexa that she had to get out of her car. The threat of fire fueled her sense of urgency, but did little to control her shaking hands as she struggled to release the seat-belt buckle.

Finally free, she steadied herself with one hand on the dashboard as she shifted her body to the left. A wave of nausea slammed into her as she started to pull herself upright, forcing her to sink back against the seat in search of renewed strength. Taking a deep breath, she tried again.

Alexa knew she wouldn't be able to stand unaided the instant she put her weight on her right leg. Pain exploded in her knee and shot up her leg. She didn't even try to restrain the cry that burst from her lips.

Dropping back into the driver's seat, she closed her eyes and released several shallow gusts of air. Dizziness swirled around her, forcing her to struggle once again for the courage and self-control she desperately needed. Determined to get as far as possible from her car, even if it meant making the trip on her hands and knees, Alexa groggily issued instructions to her uncooperative limbs.

She tried to relax enough to slide out of the driver's seat and onto the ground, but something hard and resistant stopped her as soon as she began to move. She moaned in frustration, pushed at the unexpected barrier and tried to focus on whatever stood between her and safety.

Grayson Lennox frowned as he studied the woman sprawled half in and half out of the wrecked sports car. Anchoring her in the driver's seat with one hand, he conducted a quick inventory of her features, despite her flailing arms and incoherent muttering.

"Settle down, honey," he said quietly as he studied her in the diminishing light and noted the lump already darkening her forehead and the blood seeping from the cut on her chin. "You're safe now."

"Tommy?"

Gray straightened and glanced at his ranch foreman, a weathered-looking man in his late fifties who was busy inspecting the crumpled front end of the sports car. "Make sure we haven't got another tourist wandering around out here somewhere, Will. Then take the Jeep and go get Doc Griffin. I'll take her back to the house on foot, so meet me there. We can worry about what's left of her car later."

"Sure thing, boss. Shouldn't take me more than twenty minutes."

Gray dropped to his knees beside the low-slung vehicle and carefully ran his hands over Alexa's body, checking for broken bones. He didn't want to risk compounding whatever injuries she'd already suffered when he carried her the quarter mile back to the house.

He absently noted the elegant lace gown she wore, the pallor of her skin and the enticing fragrance of her perfume. Expensive, he decided matter-of-factly, expensive from the top of what he assumed had once been an elaborate upswept hairstyle all the way down to the tips of her silk-covered toes.

Alexa flinched then moaned again when he ran his hands down her legs. Pain brought with it renewed awareness and fear. She struggled, the gesture futile as Gray easily held her still.

While Alexa mumbled in protest, Gray consciously tried to resist his memories of another accident, a fatal accident that had taken place almost a year ago. His nephew's frantic summons as he'd charged into the kitchen less than ten minutes ago, with his dog fast on his heels, yelling, "Car wreck! Car wreck!" had trapped the air in his lungs and turned the blood in his veins to sluggish rivers of ice.

Conditioned to taking responsibility for those around him, Gray forced himself to put aside his own inner turmoil, as well as his instinctive reluctance at the thought of venturing anywhere near a car wreck or its victims. Still captured by his memories, he muttered something dark and offensive under his breath.

Alexa reacted as though she'd been slapped. She instantly tried to put as much space as possible between herself and the negative sound.

Ashamed and alarmed, Gray touched her hand in what he hoped was a calming gesture. "Relax, honey. You're safe."

She heard his voice, although it sounded as though it had come from the far end of a long tunnel. "Cold." Tears crept from her eyes as she tried to hug herself for warmth.

Gray cursed himself for not recognizing the symptoms of shock. Gently lifting her out of the car, he felt her stiffen before he cradled her against his chest. Straightening his six-foot-two-inch frame, he chastised himself for not remembering what the aftereffects of an accident could do to a person's mind and body.

"I'm taking you home," he told her as he carried her. "Doc Griffin'll look you over and then we'll get you to the hospital."

Alexa relaxed somewhat, murmured something akin to assent and snuggled her arms up around his neck. Burrowing against the heat of his body, she felt a corresponding warmth infuse her own. The jeopardy she'd experienced while trapped in her car disappeared, a vague memory in a kaleidoscope of images and sensations.

What didn't disappear, however, was her nagging realization that the accident could have ended far differently, perhaps even fatally. The thought of almost dying made her tremble.

Sure-footed despite the fading light, Gray strode across the empty pasture. Alexa instinctively savored the security she found in her rescuer's arms.

He kept talking to her, his voice firm, his words resonant with reassurance. As Alexa continued to cling tightly to him, he experienced a stab of unfamiliar emotion in response to her vulnerability. It had been a long time since he'd reached out to comfort another human being. It had been even longer since a woman had needed or wanted his comfort. Suddenly uncomfortable with his role as protector, Gray picked up his pace.

"My knee," she whispered in protest, her breath rushing warmly across the side of his neck.

Gray paused and cautiously shifted her to what he hoped would be a more comfortable position. His skin still tingled from the impact of those two softly spoken words.

"Better?"

"Much," she murmured. Lucid for the first time since the accident, Alexa gingerly touched her chin, then grimaced when she felt the stickiness of her own blood on her fingertips. Her head continued to throb, but she could see clearly now.

"Think you can handle a few more minutes of being carried?"

She laughed, the sound a bit out of control and very ragged. "Beats crawling."

"That's what you were trying to do when I found you."

"I was afraid of a fire starting," she answered.

He nodded and began walking again, his booted feet and muscled frame cushioning the subtle shock of each step he took across the knee-high grass of the fenced pasture. Alexa closed her eyes and listened to the sound of his breathing. With her head resting on his shoulder, she could smell the masculine combination of leather, soap and after-shave on his skin. She smiled to herself and released a sigh.

Gray glanced down at her. A slight breeze, one still warm from the heat of the waning day, ruffled her bangs and sent them fluttering across the underside of his chin. "Are you all right?" he managed quietly.

"Just tired."

"Try to stay awake. That way the doc'll have an easier time of it when he examines you."

"Other than my knee, I guess I'm okay."

"I don't think anything's broken," Gray offered. "It felt more like pulled ligaments or maybe strained tendons, but those can hurt as much as a break."

"You sound like a doctor."

"Rancher. I breed horses."

"Mm."

"Keep talking to me, honey."

"Alexa."

"Pretty girl, pretty name."

"Woman," she corrected without thinking.

The curves of her body told him she was right. But *whose* woman? he wondered, although he knew her status wasn't any concern of his.

"Yours?"

"Grayson Lennox."

"Suits you."

He chuckled and gathered her closer. "A gift from my parents."

Sadness rippled through her and kept her from speaking. *I shouldn't have married him, I shouldn't have married him.* Her mother's words whispered through her mind again and brought fresh tears to her eyes. She swallowed the emotion knotted in her throat and exhaled softly.

Gray sensed the change in her and chalked it up to the strain of the accident. He slowed his pace and paused at the pasture gate. "Reach over and flip that latch for me so I don't have to jar your knee."

She did as he asked but remained silent. Gravel crunched under Gray's booted feet. An owl hooted in the distance, the sound oddly forlorn.

Alexa was quiet until they moved under the diffused glow of the lights that ran the length of a winding driveway. Unable to ignore the blood that had splashed across the imported lace bodice of her wedding gown, she groaned in dismay when she saw the damage.

Gray stopped abruptly, concerned that he'd somehow managed to hurt her again. Glancing down, he clenched his teeth to catch the betraying sound his surprise almost made.

The difference between her elegantly sheathed body and his faded jeans and blue chambray work shirt emphasized the dramatic contrasts of country versus city, widower versus bride and man versus woman.

Two

___

Air soundlessly escaped through Gray's gritted teeth once he permitted himself the luxury of releasing his stunned reaction to the woman cradled in his arms. He didn't say a word. Instead, he resumed his trek to the house, walking at a deceptively sedate pace as he sorted through the dozen or more questions stacking up in his mind.

Now wasn't the time. But later, he promised himself, later he would have the answers he wanted. He didn't bother to ask himself why it was necessary to know anything more about Alexa than the fact that she so dearly needed his help.

Inexplicably, he couldn't keep his curiosity at bay. Ignoring his conscience, Gray commented, "We don't get too many brides driving out this way."

"I don't imagine you do," she agreed cautiously.

"Especially not one who's alone."

"I am that."

"Alone?"

"Yes." She pressed her fingertips to her temple and massaged the persistent throbbing, the only polite way she could think of to retreat from conversation.

Senses alert to the tension that had sifted into Alexa's body, he didn't push her any further. He rounded the final bend in the driveway and stepped onto the sprawling stretch of manicured lawn that fronted his home. His housekeeper, a retired schoolteacher and the wife of his ranch foreman, stood expectantly on the porch.

As soon as Gray climbed the wide porch steps, the older woman opened the double oak front doors of the three-story house and moved aside. Alexa heard her fall into step behind them as Gray carried her down a long hallway.

Despite her injuries, she couldn't ignore the gleaming hardwood floors or the lemon wax that scented the air of Grayson Lennox's home. Victorian by design, the house possessed a subtle elegance and masculine simplicity unlike the frilly feminine decor so common among the bed-and-breakfast inns of Santa Barbara.

She also noticed the rooms that opened onto the hallway. Although her impressions were somewhat fleeting, she mentally cataloged the floor-to-ceiling bookshelves that lined the walls of a well-stocked library, a formal dining area dominated by a long oak trestle table and flanked by several wing chairs, and a spacious living room.

"Will just called. He said to tell you that he and Doc Griffin'll be along soon." The housekeeper hesitated briefly and then continued, "Michael's had his dinner. He's upstairs in his room now."

"Thanks, Minna."

With his housekeeper trailing along after them, Gray carried Alexa up a flight of stairs to a room at the end of the second-floor hallway. The older woman preceded them, reaching for a light switch as she entered the guest room.

The shade-covered bulb of a bedside lamp illuminated the room, bathing it in a soft glow.

Crossing the spacious room, Gray carefully lowered Alexa to the edge of an antique brass bed covered with a hunter-green satin spread. "Minna, this is Alexa…" He paused and waited for her to supply her last name. He would have the answer to that, at least.

"Alexa Rivers," she confirmed, vaguely aware of the not-so-subtle machinations of her host.

"Well, miss, let's see if we can get you settled in before Doc gets here."

"Call me Alexa, please."

Minna smiled approvingly and rounded the end of the bed. She came to a stop beside Alexa before glancing at Gray. Lost in private thought, he finally noticed the expectant looks on the faces of both women. He turned on his heel and left the room. Alexa didn't miss his abrupt mood change, but she didn't have the energy to try to figure out the cause.

"Why don't we get you out of your dress?" Minna asked, compassion evident in her voice.

Alexa nodded and set to work on the tiny satin-covered buttons on the sleeves of her gown. The pain in her shoulder made movement of any kind difficult, and she appreciated the housekeeper's deft efficiency when she relieved her of the task.

Minna paused after loosening the buttons of both sleeves and the back of the fitted gown. "If you can stand up for just a moment, we'll pretend you're a banana and peel this little number right off you."

Alexa smiled faintly and, with Minna's help, managed to stand and put the majority of her weight on her left leg. Between the two of them, they eased the wedding gown, as well as her panty hose, over the gentle flare of her hips and down her slim legs. Blood-spattered ice-white French lace and satin pooled at her feet. She sank back onto the bed, still clad in a modest ankle-length full slip.

The older woman retrieved the discarded gown. The expression on Alexa's face prompted her to comment, "It may take a bit of work, but I should be able to get the blood out."

Alexa felt a chill run up her spine and hugged herself for warmth. "Some things just aren't meant to be."

The housekeeper nodded but didn't say anything. Humming softly to herself, she crossed the room, drew back floor-to-ceiling drapes and opened two doors, which led out onto a second-floor balcony that extended the entire length of the back of the house. The rich smell of wild honeysuckle drifted into the room on a slow moving wave of sultry summer night air.

Alexa soon found a comfortable position on the bed and gratefully eased her battered upper body onto an array of throw pillows scattered against the intricate design of the brass headboard. When the housekeeper slipped into the adjoining bathroom, she took the opportunity to study her surroundings.

Walls painted the palest shade of cream contrasted dramatically with the hunter-green bedspread and drapes. Two wing chairs separated by an elegantly carved, marble-topped oval table, an enormous teak bureau with ornate brass drawer pulls, and a collection of framed pastoral scenes arranged on the walls, gave the room the ambience of a bygone era.

Minna returned just as a door in the lower regions of the house slammed shut. "That'll be Will and Doc Griffin."

"Thank you for your help."

"No need to thank me, miss. Grayson's offered you his hospitality, and that's good enough for me. Don't worry now, Doc'll fix you up better than new. And there are plenty of fresh towels in the bathroom, if you need them later."

Caught in a web of her own thoughts, Alexa nodded. She couldn't stop wondering if the child she'd seen just before the accident lived at the ranch. Worried about him, she gave in to her curiosity. "Who's Michael?"

Minna looked startled but quickly recovered. "Grayson's nephew. His sister's boy."

"He lives here?"

"For the summer. Grayson's parents decided it was time."

Alexa didn't know what to make of the housekeeper's final remark. The sound of footsteps coming down the hall, Grayson Lennox's distinctive booted stride and the less dominant sounds of softer-soled shoes, prevented further comment by either woman.

Minna retrieved a lightweight blanket from an old seaman's chest positioned near the end of the bed and placed it on the quilt beside Alexa. "I'll find a bed jacket for you once Doc leaves."

Gray and Dr. Griffin hesitated outside the door. Alexa felt a rush of relief when the doctor came in alone, a capable look on his mature face and a battered leather medical bag gripped in his hand. He examined her with practiced ease, his comments and questions medical in nature, his touch gentle but firm and his curiosity, if he had any, well concealed.

After tucking the blanket around his patient, he patted her shoulder and called out, "You can come in now, Gray. No need to pace that hallway like an expectant father."

Alexa, amused by the doctor's characterization of her host, listened in amazement as the two men proceeded to discuss the current state of her health. Discussed it and her, she realized, without a thought to the fact that she was even in the room.

"Keep her off that right leg. She's wrenched it good, torn some ligaments and strained the tendons. It'll be a while before she can safely walk on it. Meanwhile, our patient needs lots of rest, Minna's good cooking and pain pills starting tomorrow for her knee if she wants them. As far as tonight's concerned,'' he lectured, ''I don't want her left alone.''

''Concussion?'' Gray asked with the same intensity Alexa had heard and seen earlier.

She watched her host's facial expression while she absorbed the doctor's instructions. Why was he so concerned about her? She didn't understand him, and she didn't understand his interest. She also didn't understand why her pulse leaped at the very sight of him.

''A mild concussion and probably nothing to worry about, but better safe than sorry. Keep a close eye on her, wake her every few hours, check her pupils and keep her off that leg. No need to take her to the hospital for stitches. The butterfly bandage I used'll keep her from having much more than a hairline scar.''

''Dr. Griffin?''

Both men looked surprised by her interruption.

''Yes?''

''When will I be well enough to drive?''

''You won't be for at least a few weeks,'' he told her. ''If you get into a car and try to drive before it's time, you'll end up having orthopedic surgery. The choice is yours, young woman,'' he warned gruffly. ''Besides, if that was your car I saw wrapped around Gray's corner oak, then you won't be driving for a while, anyway.''

Gray and Dr. Griffin both saw the shock in her eyes. Gray moved toward her, more out of instinct than by design. Doc continued talking, this time to his patient, although his eyes followed Gray's protective movements. Apparently pleased by what he saw, he smiled.

"You're in good hands here, miss. I've known Gray all his life, and I'm friends with his folks. If you're worried about your family, I can tell them and—"

"No, there's no one to call," she hastened to assure them. The effort of looking at the two men, who now stood on opposite sides of the bed, aggravated the pounding already going on in her head.

"Any problems, get on the phone or send Will over for me," Doc Griffin admonished.

Gray shot him a look that expressed his irritation at being cautioned about such an obvious course of action should an emergency arise. "Of course."

Alexa saw the look, too, and decided it would have electrocuted a lesser man. She also interpreted it as Gray Lennox's annoyance at being saddled with an unexpected guest. As much as she hated to admit it to herself, she would have to get in touch with her father in the morning. She couldn't bring herself to impose on the indefinite hospitality of a stranger, especially since she no longer felt welcome in his home.

Alexa nearly jumped off the bed when she felt a hand on her shoulder. Eyes wide, she stared up at Gray.

He frowned at her tenseness. "Take it easy now and quit worrying. I'll be back in a few minutes. Try and rest while I'm gone."

"Somehow, I don't think I've got much choice in the matter," she replied, confused by the disparity of his hard looks and kind words.

Doc Griffin wished her a peaceful night and told them both that he would stop by in a day or two. Gray escorted him from the room.

Alexa again sank back against the pillows, tiredly closed her eyes and pondered her alternatives. Driving on to Lake Tahoe was no longer an option, nor was driving anywhere.

She immediately discarded the idea of calling Tom, primarily because she hoped he'd used his airline ticket and gone ahead to the Caribbean. After dealing with her father, Alexa was sure he needed an extended vacation.

Frustrated with the entire situation, Alexa abandoned her thoughts and opened her eyes. Instead of an empty room, she saw a boy of about seven or eight. He stood beside the bed, his brow furrowed with concern and his white-knuckled hands clasped together in front of him. His pale hair, which had acted as a beacon on the road, confirmed his identity.

They stared at one another for several moments. During those quiet seconds, Alexa experienced a variety of emotions. Compassion dominated.

Sensing that he wouldn't speak first, she decided to break the ice. Being examined like a bug trapped in a fruit jar held little appeal, anyway. "Hello."

"You're not mad at me, are you? Did any of your bones get broken? Are you gonna be okay?"

Taken aback by his rapid-fire delivery, Alexa reached out, grasped his knotted hands and tugged him forward. She silently urged him to sit on the edge of the bed by patting the top of the satin spread, then waited while he overcame his reluctance.

Neither Alexa nor the boy realized that Gray now stood, still and silent, just outside the partially open guest room door. He'd returned to the second floor quietly, certain that Alexa had probably fallen asleep by now.

"You're Michael, aren't you?" she asked.

He nodded with the energy typical of his age group. He nodded so vigorously that the bed began to shake. Alexa flinched and shifted her knee.

"I knew you'd be mad at me," he whispered, worried when he saw her grimace.

"No, Michael, I'm not angry," she assured him. "I haven't got any broken bones, and I'll be fine in a few weeks. I just wrenched my knee and gave myself a heck of a headache.''

"You've got a big bump on your forehead. I had one of those once." He looked around nervously then returned his thickly lashed dark eyes, eyes that reminded Alexa of his uncle, to her face. "I saw all that blood on your chin. I thought you were going to die and it would've been my fault. Crackers and me didn't mean to make you wreck your car. Honest, we didn't.''

"I believe you."

Standing in the hallway, Gray struggled to contain his racing thoughts and the emotion whirling inside him. Closing his hands into tight fists, he made himself listen, made himself try to understand, even though Michael's admission of responsibility for a serious car accident was like a hammer blow to his soul.

Wasn't it enough that he had to live with his *own* demons? Why had his parents insisted that Michael spend the summer at Lennox Ranch? He knew the answer, of course, but he didn't want to think about their reasoning right now. Hell, he didn't want to think about the last four years of his life.

And he definitely didn't want to be around anyone who reminded him of the multiple tragedies or the anguish he had endured during those four years. Not even Michael, his godson, and his own sole responsibility if anything happened to Gray's parents, the boy's current legal guardians. He loved his sister's only child, but he was a constant and painful reminder to Gray of her death.

"Crackers was chasing a rabbit," Michael explained. "He just took off."

"And you took off after him?"

When he didn't say anything, Alexa noted his intent study of the toes of his sneakers. His behavior reminded her of the kids at Rivers House. She felt a smile tug at the edges of her mouth.

"My mom and dad died in a car wreck," he suddenly blurted out. "A drunk driver crashed into us. I got hurt, too. It was real scary."

Gray jerked his head up as though dodging the closed fist of an assailant. Still, he remained at the door and kept his silent vigil.

Alexa, still dealing with the emotional extremes of the day, mentally flashed on the pain she'd felt when her own mother had died, as well as the isolation she had experienced. Her heart went out to Michael.

"Car wrecks *are* scary," she agreed softly. "It's hard to be brave when you feel like your world's been turned upside down."

"Wow! Something like that's happened to you, too?"

"Something similar, Michael," she agreed. Her eyelids grew heavy, won the short battle she tried to wage and fell closed.

"You all right?"

She almost groaned. "Now you sound like your uncle."

"Really?"

Alexa cracked open one eye. Michael seemed inordinately pleased by her observation. Hero worship, she concluded.

"I gotta go. I'm supposed to be in my room studying. I have school stuff to make up this summer."

She smiled. "Then maybe we should both do what we're supposed to do."

"Can I come and see you again?"

"How about tomorrow morning?"

"And you're sure you're not mad at me?" he asked again as he slid off the bed and moved toward the balcony doors.

"I'm not mad. Just promise me you'll be more careful the next time you and Crackers are out near the road."

"I promise," floated in the air behind him as he slipped out the double doors.

Alexa sighed softly and tugged the blanket up to her shoulders. She liked Michael, although it bothered her a little that he reminded her of some of the lonely children she knew at Rivers House.

Gray made a split-second decision about Alexa and his nephew before taking a deep, steadying breath. Unclenching his fists, he silently cursed the tremor he noticed in his hand as he rapped on the guest room door.

Not bothering to wait for an invitation, he pushed it open, strode across the room, stopped beside the head of the bed and leaned down. "Put your arms around me and I'll help you up. Minna's bringing you a dinner tray."

Too startled by his sudden appearance and too hungry to refuse a meal, Alexa complied with his order. She noticed the stern look on his face and almost apologized for being such an inconvenience, but she balked at actually saying the words. Being treated like an accomplice in a crime before all the facts were known annoyed her. Instead, she silently accepted his help.

Gray consciously fought his response to the beckoning scent of her perfume, the vulnerability in her large eyes and the bandage taped across the bottom half of her chin. He might have been successful had the blanket covering Alexa not slipped.

His fingers tightened convulsively on her back when he saw the bruise that had spread across her shoulder and down her left arm. An angry shade of purple, the color matched the knot on her forehead, marring otherwise flawless peach-toned skin.

Against his will, his gaze slid lower. Alexa's smooth, toned flesh, and the erratic rise and fall of her breasts beneath the lace bodice of her slip, teased his senses and tensed every centimeter of already hard muscle in his lean male body.

He dragged piercing dark eyes back up to her face with tremendous effort. The stunned look on her face and the rush of color tinting her cheeks nudged him back to reality.

His nephew needed this woman. She was the first person he'd warmed to since his mother's death. She might be able to help him, Gray reminded himself. The remainder served as a warning not to do anything stupid, especially not now.

The air around them grew turbulent. Alexa stopped breathing. She stared at Gray, eyes wide and nerves strung as tightly as piano wire. She couldn't seem to pull her gaze from the hard line of his jaw or the shadowy stubble that wanted shaving. Nor could she ignore the musky smell of his skin.

She sensed that he could and would overpower her under different circumstances, although not in a physically hurtful way. His power was far greater, far more threatening, because he touched off sparks in places inside her that she hadn't even realized could be combustible.

He smiled suddenly, his teeth even rows of white that contrasted sharply against his darkly tanned face. The action softened his strong chin and cut slashing grooves into the skin just below his taut cheeks. It also made Alexa feel as though she'd just taken a ride on a speeding comet.

"Take a breath," he suggested. "Oxygen starvation isn't a pretty sight."

She blinked, did as he instructed, then could have happily kicked herself for being so witless. Bewildered and still breathless, Alexa cocked her head questioningly.

Gray drew back and stepped away from the bed. She reminded him of a wary little fox, one who scents danger but is also curious about the source. Forcing himself to walk across the room, he stood beside the tall teak bureau. A full minute passed before he trusted his voice. "Relax, Alexa. I'm not going to hurt you."

She wondered about that, and she also wondered about his sudden use of her name. *Honey* had suited his purposes until now. "What *are* you going to do?"

"That remains to be seen."

"*What* exactly remains to be seen?" she asked, feeling out of sync with him, the conversation and the entire planet.

"How I handle your stay at Lennox Ranch."

"There's nothing to handle."

"I don't agree, and since this is my home, I suspect I'll have the final say in the matter."

Alexa pressed her fingertips to her forehead and sighed. "Look, I'll make arrangements to leave in the morning. We're both smart enough to realize that it doesn't matter where I recuperate, just as long as I follow the doctor's instructions about my knee. My departure should solve all the problems I've managed to cause in the last few hours. If you'll let me know the cost of repairing the fence I damaged, I'd be happy to pay the bill."

Gray shook his head, abandoned what had developed into directionless pacing around the spacious room and came to a stop at the foot of the brass bed. His wide-legged stance and the expression on his face were purposely intimidating. He needed Alexa's attention, and he didn't plan to be shy about using any tool at his disposal in order to get it.

"Everything's already taken care of. Your car's being towed to a garage in Jackson, your luggage is downstairs in the front hall, and you'll stay here at the ranch until you can get around on your own."

"Wait a minute!" she cried, alarmed by his take-charge attitude.

"Wait for what?" Gray asked. "Wait for you to fall asleep, because you're so exhausted you're having trouble keeping your eyes open? Wait for you to accept the fact that you can't move around under your own steam and need a place to stay? Or should I wait while you waste time searching for a solution to a problem I've already solved?"

She glared at him, fighting both fatigue and outrage at being so skillfully managed. Shades of her father, she thought in disgust. Anger renewed her energy. "Mr. Lennox, I'm capable of taking care of myself."

"Like you did on the road tonight?" he challenged, although he knew the truth of the matter.

Gray mentally justified his question by weighing his admittedly aggressive behavior against the desperation he felt with Michael. *She had to stay.* It was the first idea that had made any sense to him in the three weeks since his nephew's arrival at the ranch.

"What happened to me was an accident. I lost control of my car. It happens."

"Does it?" He silently applauded her response, knowing that her protective instincts would benefit Michael.

"Yes, it does!" She winced when she heard her own words echo sharply in her head.

"Does this mean you don't want my help?"

"You're already helping me," she pointed out. Alexa noticed the subtle shifting of muscle beneath his shirt each time he took a breath of air. She briefly closed her eyes to block out the sight of him and then tried a more diplomatic approach. "I really appreciate what you've done for me, Mr. Lennox, but you and your family don't need me underfoot."

Gray sauntered toward her like some long-legged, lean-hipped cowboy striding out of the sunset, rather than riding off into it. He towered over her as he stood beside the head of the bed. She held very still, eyes narrowed and limbs tensed.

"Call me Gray. Appreciation isn't the issue, as far as I'm concerned. But what *does* concern me is the financial stability of my ranch and the possibility that you could easily decide to sue me for damages some hotshot Santa Barbara lawyer might decide to dream up on your behalf.''

Stunned, she could only stare. He'd either checked her car registration or discovered the identification she carried in her purse. She couldn't decide which, although her sense of fair play made her settle on the former. She couldn't picture him rifling a woman's purse.

Gray toned down his ire when he saw Alexa's reaction to his comments. ''What also concerns me is the eight-year-old kid you've managed to frighten, the fence line you've destroyed and the damage to a pasture my pregnant mares use, not to mention what you've done to yourself.''

His voice softened even more before he launched his final salvo, but his message didn't change. ''I feel responsible for you, Alexa Rivers, so get yourself used to the idea of staying put until I'm sure you'll be all right.''

She opened her mouth to speak, but Minna sailed through the open door carrying a dinner tray. Alexa pressed her lips together in frustration. The housekeeper stopped beside the bed, her expression benign despite the argument Alexa was certain she'd overheard.

''I've brought you a bowl of chicken soup, a dish of sliced fresh peaches and a cup of herbal tea. Doc said you're to eat sparingly until tomorrow morning, but I promise to fix you a bona fide country breakfast as soon as you wake up. Think you're ready for a little snack now?''

Alexa didn't intend to disappoint the housekeeper or her stomach. She also needed a respite from Gray Lennox, and she definitely needed a few minutes to figure out how she was going to deal with him.

Smoothing down the blanket that had gotten bunched around her waist, she accepted the tray. ''This looks wonderful, Minna.''

The older woman beamed at her, gave Gray a severe look and departed. Alexa missed the silent exchange between the two.

"Eat your meal, then we'll finish talking." He dropped into a chair near the balcony doors as he spoke, his long legs stretched out in front of him. His relaxed posture belied a tense body and racing thoughts.

Alexa ignored him, popped a slice of peach into her mouth and chewed, slowly and deliberately. Gray grinned when he saw her attempt to dismiss him. He liked her spirit. And he liked *her*, despite how little he knew about her.

She ate at a leisurely pace, savoring the first meal she'd had all day. She didn't appreciate her host's high-handed behavior or his continued presence in the room, but she knew she couldn't really do much about him or his attitude.

Ten silent minutes ticked by. Alexa finally refolded her napkin and placed it beside the empty soup bowl. "If you'll excuse me, Mr. Lennox, I need to get some sleep. In the morning I'll make whatever arrangements are necessary to insure that I'll be gone by midday. I will also pay for the inconvenience I've caused you and, as I said earlier, the damage I've done to your pasture fence. Draw up a document that absolves you of any and all responsibility for the accident, and I'll sign it. With witnesses, of course."

She smiled at him, feeling that she'd finally gotten the upper hand. "And that, Mr. Lennox, will be the end of the matter. I'm sure you now realize that there isn't anything left for us to discuss. Thank you again for your help," she concluded formally.

Alexa slid the tray onto the nightstand, settled back against the pillows after tugging up the blanket and closed her eyes. She clenched her fists and swore in silent fury when she heard him chuckle.

"Get some sleep, Alexa. I'll be here if you need anything during the night."

On that less than soothing note, Alexa forced herself to concentrate on relaxing enough to fall asleep. She didn't expect to rest at all, but she fell into a fitful doze almost immediately.

True to his word, Gray remained with her throughout the night.

He left the muted light of the bedside lamp on so that Alexa wouldn't be alarmed if she awoke. He checked her every two hours and was surprised by her trusting acceptance of his need to disturb her sleep.

She routinely pushed aside the blanket draped over her willowy body. He routinely retrieved it and re-covered her.

He often lingered during those moments, studying the delicate curve of her brow or gathering her into his arms when she seemed tormented by her dreams. When doing the latter, he told himself that he was only trying to help her.

Gray slept in short spurts in the wing chair when fatigue claimed him. The discomfort of having his long limbs restricted by the shape of the chair invariably wakened him, though, prompting him to stand, stretch the kinks from his large body and wander out onto the balcony.

Welcomed by the soft scents and familiar sounds of the night, he found he didn't mind his role as sentry. It gave him time to plan what he knew would be the next round with Alexa, but only when he wasn't torturing himself with thoughts of her sprawled, naked and willing, across his bed in the master suite at the opposite end of the hallway.

The intelligence and stubbornness he'd already seen in her blue-gray eyes, eyes that were enormous and fringed with impossibly dark lashes given her fair skin and glowing hair, assured him that she would be a worthy adversary. But he had need on his side, and need often translated into positive action if the cause was valid.

Gray briefly left his post just before dawn. As he stripped off his clothes and climbed into the shower, he assured himself that his decision to ask her to remain at the ranch was the right one. He then reminded himself that he hadn't exactly *asked* Alexa Rivers to do anything.

His conscience gnawed at him. He decided to lay his cards on the table as soon as the time was right. Then he would ask her to stay while her knee healed. A few weeks, maybe longer. By then he would have his feelings about his nephew straightened out. The boy deserved more than an emotional cripple for an uncle.

After shaving, dressing and pulling on his boots, Gray returned to the guest room. He walked into the room, instantly lost his temper and swore so viciously that Alexa froze in midhop.

Three

———

With an economy of movement amazing in so large a man, Gray had Alexa off her uninjured leg and in his arms before she could close her shock-slackened mouth or even think of easing her trembling body back down to the edge of the bed.

He held her to his chest, taking care not to jostle her bad knee. "You heard what Doc Griffin said, so will you quit acting like you don't have the sense God gave a termite?"

She stiffened. "Don't badger me, Mr. Lennox, and put me down."

"Think again, honey. When you need help, ask for it. Otherwise, I'll post a guard. If you don't follow Doc's orders, you'll wind up under a surgeon's knife."

She knew he was right, but she stubbornly refused to admit it. The man put her nerves on edge; the discomfort she now felt managed to hone them to razor sharpness. "I don't need your help."

"Don't you?" he asked ever so softly.

Stubbornness and pride cleaved inside her. "No."

Despite her feistiness, or maybe even because of it, he felt shockingly possessive of her. He didn't appreciate the powerful emotion.

"Look at me, Alexa."

She heard the softening in his voice, but decided it was a ruse of some kind. He was smooth and bossy and unpredictable, and too much like her father. Manipulative in the extreme.

"Alexa?"

She reluctantly lifted her eyes. "What?"

"I'm just trying to help you."

"I don't trust you," she announced, then bit her lip at her own bluntness. Had she left her manners in her wrecked car?

He smiled. "I don't imagine you do. And it's mostly my fault. I'm sorry."

Startled, she didn't know what to think, with him changing so much from one minute to the next. Disarmed by his behavior and distracted by their close proximity to one another, she studied him with a frankness that would have normally left her feeling amazed at her own rudeness.

Gray didn't budge under her scrutiny. He simply watched her with that steady gaze of his. If this was her way of deciding on his trustworthiness, then he would meet her needs.

Alexa's eyes swept across his face. She mapped a strong chin, high cheekbones, a nose that had suffered and endured the fists of another, large, thickly lashed dark brown eyes and slashing dark brows like an experienced surveyor.

But it was his close-cropped dark hair that caught her attention and held it. It was still damp from his shower, and she could see the marks his comb had made in the mink-thick pelt. The sight intrigued her, made her fingers itch with the desire to reach out and test both texture and substance. She sighed, the sound audible and quite involuntary.

He inhaled sharply. "Don't look at me that way. It makes me hungry for things I shouldn't want and can't have."

She flushed at his directness and glanced at her hands. "I need to use the bathroom."

Gray blinked, surprised by her hurried words. "Is that why you got up by yourself?"

What a subject! She nodded.

"Then just say so next time," he ordered, the boss again. "Bodily functions are a natural part of life. They don't offend me, and they shouldn't offend you."

"Don't lecture me," she snapped, unable to keep herself from being snippy. All she wanted was a long soak in a hot tub and a lot of privacy, not some sexy-looking rancher orchestrating her every move.

She also wanted to leave Lennox Ranch. Too many issues needed resolution before she could return to Santa Barbara. Being here certainly wasn't conducive to the peace of mind necessary to rethink her relationship with her father or to figure out the best way to handle the future.

"Didn't you think I was coming back?" he asked, his tone of voice once again subdued as he carried her into the adjoining bathroom.

She didn't say anything.

"Alexa, I'm not leaving you alone until you answer me."

She raised eyes filled with sparks of rebellion. "I woke up when I heard you leave. I didn't know what to think."

Amazed, he shook his head and carefully lowered her so that she could place her weight on her left leg and use the sink top for support. In spite of her admission, he didn't think for a minute that she was insecure, not with that temper of hers. "Call me when you're ready to be carried back to bed."

Frustrated that he was back to his order-everybody-around behavior again, she simply nodded and kept her eyes on the sink until she heard the door click shut. She ran water full force into the basin while she attended to her needs, then felt like an idiot for resorting to such obvious subterfuge.

Five minutes later, Gray found her in the same position he had left her in. Handing her a short white terry robe, one of his own, he helped her put it on then carried her back into the bedroom. His matter-of-fact behavior made Alexa feel less self-conscious, but only slightly.

Intent on giving her a look at her surroundings, Gray nudged open one of the balcony doors with the toe of his booted foot and stepped out onto the balcony. The sun had just begun its advance across the land, blazingly strong despite the early hour.

"Minna will be up in a little while," he explained. "Meantime, I'll bring your luggage up for you. You can bathe and get into your own clothes. If I remember correctly, that kind of thing's important to a woman." The look on his face said he thought the whole notion was silly. "But don't even think about climbing into the tub unless Minna's here to help you."

Alexa gaped at him until she found her tongue. "Will you stop with all the orders? I'm not one of your ranch hands. Try and remember that, as well as what I told you last night. I'm just passing through."

He continued as if she hadn't spoken. "You'll have breakfast within the hour, then you can get back to sleep. You need a lot of rest. Doc thinks you're a bit on the puny side. I agree, but after a few weeks of Minna's cooking, you'll look a heck of a lot better. In fact—"

"Stop telling me what, when and how to do things!" Alexa nearly shouted, interrupting him. "And I'm not *puny*. I just have small bones."

"Temper, temper, Alexa," he teased. "You're way too young to start sounding like a shrew."

"I'll be twenty-four next month, if it's any concern of yours. And I don't sound like a shrew. I sound like a woman who's sick to death of everyone telling her how to live her life."

His expression hardened. "Maybe you ought to listen once in a while. It might save you a whole lot of aggravation in the future, not to mention being laid up with a bad knee from reckless driving." Gray said the last out of sheer orneriness and knew it. The spitting little cat would drive him nuts in two minutes if he let her.

"Read my lips, Mr. Lennox—"

"Gray," he inserted calmly.

She ignored him. "I'm not staying."

"That remains to be seen." He carried her into the guest room, abandoning his plan to show her the land behind the house as the sun sought lodging in the morning sky.

"Put me down."

He glanced at her, shocked by the low fury in her voice. "No way, honey. You couldn't even crawl across the room if you had to."

She knew he was right, but it galled her to even consider admitting it. "Don't bully me, *Gray*," she warned, emphasizing his name. "It's the sign of a shallow personality and a weak mind when a person has to govern those around him like a dictator. I've lived with that mentality all my life, and I'm finished putting up with it. So either put me in that bed and let me think for myself, or drive me to the edge of your property and leave me there. Whatever decision you make, I'll deal with it, but quit ordering me around like some brainless twit because it suits your needs and flatters your ego to manipulate people."

"Feel better?" he asked mildly as he lowered her to the bed and arranged the blanket over her legs.

"Better than I've felt in months," she answered, more than a little ashamed of her tirade.

"I must've hit a pretty big nerve."

She reacted to his unexpected compassion by admitting, "A major nerve. It's called my life, but I'm working on it. And please don't be kind. I doubt that I deserve either your kindness or your hospitality just now."

Gray sat down on the edge of the bed after making certain Alexa's right leg was positioned so that it wouldn't be jarred by the give of the mattress. He watched her massage the tension between her brows.

"I think we've managed to clear the air, don't you?"

She nodded but couldn't bring herself to do more than glance at him.

"I don't want you out of this bed without help. Me, Will or Minna. Take your choice, but call for help first. Otherwise, I'm serious about having somebody in here around the clock. Agreed?" He saw helplessness and frustration darken her eyes when she swung her gaze to his face and glared at him. "I'll stand guard over you myself twenty-four hours a day if I have to," he warned tersely.

She had already decided not to risk hurting herself again, but she still bristled at his tone. "Agreed, but only if you stop coming on to me like some kind of human bulldozer. It reminds me too much of... of someone I know."

Gray, conscious of the fact that he could now afford to be gracious, accepted her condition. Almost. "All right, but only as long as you follow Doc's orders." At least she wasn't still talking about leaving by midday.

"I was serious when I said I wouldn't be staying."

Gray exhaled heavily. "Compromise with me. Stay a few days and see how you feel about things then."

"But why?"

He saw her confusion and uncertainty and reached for her hand. "Just humor me, Alexa. In a couple of days you'll be stronger physically, we'll know what kind of repairs your car's going to need, and I'll feel like I've helped you as much as I can." He didn't add that he needed her help with his nephew. That little announcement, he decided, would be a case of too much, too soon.

"Let me think about it," she suggested, feeling oddly like she was looking a gift horse in the mouth.

He made himself accept her hesitation, despite the nearly overwhelming urge to try to coerce her into agreeing with his idea that she should cooperate fully with him. "I can accept that—for now."

She shot him a look that said he'd better.

Gray started to stand, but before getting to his feet he turned, reached out and placed his fingertips on Alexa's cheek. He saw the startled widening of her eyes and heard the swift intake of her breath.

"Are you married or not?" he asked, his voice vibrating with unexpected intensity.

"No," she whispered, stunned by his abrupt verbal left turn. "I couldn't go through with it."

He muttered something that sounded vaguely like, "Thank God for small favors," but Alexa was too disconcerted by his original question to be sure.

"I don't think—" she began.

"Then don't, just rest. That's all you need to do for the time being."

Gray still hadn't taken his hand from her face. Instead of doing the prudent thing and walking away from the temptation she posed, he closed his eyes, pressed the flat of his hand to her cheek and extended his long fingers so that they drove deep channels into the tumbled thickness of her hair. He inhaled deeply, filling his lungs with the faint jasmine scent of her skin as he savored the silken texture of the strands of hair trickling between his fingers.

Alexa held very still, although the urge to press her face into the callused warmth of Gray's palm surged through her. She forced herself to remember that he was a stranger, a bossy, arrogant and overbearing stranger determined to manage and manipulate her.

"Mr. Lennox?"

"Gray," he reminded her as he opened his eyes and studied her shocked features.

"Gray," she repeated, virtually hypnotized by the look in his eyes and the expression on his face. "You shouldn't—"

He shook his head. "Don't, Alexa."

"But—"

"Please."

She nodded, only vaguely aware of her own surrender. If she let herself, she could easily fall victim to his fathomless dark eyes—eyes that seemed to challenge and seduce simultaneously.

Instinct assured her that Grayson Lennox was roughedged, untamed and dangerous—especially to someone like her. He exuded an understated yet totally natural masculine aura that few men ever achieved. Her common sense urged her to flee. Alexa shivered, as much from the realization of his personal power as from the scorching heat of his gaze.

If this were another time or another place, and if he were any other man, she sensed that she would have welcomed the unexpected emotions churning inside her. But not here, and definitely not now. Too much needed fixing in her life to complicate it further.

Gray ran his thumb across the fullness of her lower lip, the urge to taste her flourishing inside him as he punished himself with the erotic images racing through his mind. Alexa Rivers made him think things he had no right to think and want things he had no right to want.

He abruptly jerked his hand from her face, stood, turned on his heel and walked out of the room, leaving a trembling Alexa to deal with the memory of both his presumptive arrogance and his devastating tenderness.

Alexa spent the majority of her first two days at Lennox Ranch either sleeping or being fussed over by Minna when she wasn't the recipient of visits from Gray's nephew. She abandoned the idea of a speedy departure as soon as she awoke that first morning. Already stiff and bruised from the accident and with her knee feeling as though a hot poker had been wedged into it, she didn't have the strength or the inclination to try to arrange a return trip to Santa Barbara. But she did try to contact Tom. His secretary informed her that he was on vacation and wouldn't be back for three weeks.

She remained unaware of how often her host checked on her, because he confined his queries to his housekeeper and to silent forays up to the guest room when he was certain Alexa was asleep.

Young Michael's visits were brief but frequent, his arrival in her room normally coinciding with the delivery of a meal tray. A likable little boy, he never ran short of things to say.

She encouraged the eight-year-old to talk, unaware that she was providing him with a conversational outlet he hadn't enjoyed since the death of his parents the previous summer. She felt an odd sense of kinship with Michael and empathized with his need to share his memories, something she herself hadn't been able to do with anyone, especially not her father, after her mother's death.

Minna seemed determined to rectify the doctor's observation that his patient was too thin for her size. Alexa delighted in the variety and quality of the nourishment offered her, but the pain pills she sparingly took for her knee di-

minished her normally healthy appetite. She also appreciated the older woman's help when bathing and dressing,
despite the fact that all she did was exchange one nightgown for another whenever she freshened up.

Still unnerved by the disturbing emotions she'd already
experienced because of Gray, she used the hours she spent
alone to rest, collect her wits and consider her personal options for the future. She credited Gray's absence to the demands of running his ranch, while comments made in
passing by Minna confirmed that his days generally started
at dawn and often didn't end until midnight.

Two days and four hours following Alexa's arrival at the
ranch, Gray left his office and returned to the main house.
A soft rain dampened his face and lightning from a summer storm in the distant mountains flashed silently across
the black velvet of the night sky as he walked the flagstone
path to the kitchen door.

Fatigue now dominated his body, but desire had driven
him at a relentless pace throughout most of the last two
days.

Quietly making his way through the still house, he
stopped briefly at the bar in the library and poured himself
a brandy before climbing the stairs to the second-floor hallway. He paused at the entrance to the master suite when he
heard Alexa cry out.

Wrenched from a restless sleep by her vivid dreams, Alexa
reached for the bedside lamp. She encountered warm flesh
and shrank back against the pillows, confused and frightened as she floundered in the twilight zone between sleep
and wakefulness.

Gray switched on the light and reached for her. She
moved into his arms, accepting his comfort without hesitation or thought. He held her gently, conscious of her trembling body and the terror that still held her in its thrall.

Hunger, powerful and startling, lanced through him as he soothed her with reassuring words and the steady stroking of his hands moving easily up and down the length of her narrow back.

He longed to touch her in the same way any man aches to touch a woman who has, however unintentionally, reached into his soul and made him feel the burning intensity of denied desire.

Reason, and her obvious vulnerability, however, told him he could not.

He longed to know the heady pleasure of her naked flesh entwined with his. He longed to press his face to her bare skin and inhale once again the intoxicating scent of wild jasmine on a spring breeze, a scent he now knew would stay with him into eternity.

He longed to know that her heart could beat out of control because of him. And he longed to go beyond the lace now covering her body and experience what he was certain was the rose-petal softness of her skin, skin he suspected could just as easily take on the texture of hot silk in the throes of passion.

Reason, and the shattering depth of her trust, warned him of the danger of fantasizing.

Still, he visualized running his hands the length of her body, lingering so that he could leisurely explore her full breasts, the tapering slimness of her narrow waist and softly flaring hips that even now innocently enticed. When his mind created an image of her long, slim legs wrapped around his lower torso, he nearly groaned aloud.

Reason intruded one final time and jerked him back to reality. With it came an instinctive understanding of what it would do to them both if he somehow betrayed her trust or compromised the integrity that he valued in himself.

Alexa felt the tension invading Gray's body. Lifting her head from his shoulder, she studied him, worry in her eyes and a frown marring her brow.

Gray swiftly brought himself under control. He was a grown man, old enough, at thirty-four, he reminded himself harshly, not to give in to his body's urges. He'd never in his life taken advantage of anyone who was hurting and vulnerable. And this big-eyed woman with her fiery-gold hair and frightened expression was both.

He released her, retrieved the brandy snifter and got to his feet, wandering toward the double doors that opened out onto the balcony as his heartbeat slowed and his senses calmed.

"Bad dreams?" he finally asked, his back still to her.

"I guess so, but I can't remember them now."

"How's your head?"

"It doesn't hurt anymore."

Alexa saw his weariness as he leaned against the door frame, working the muscles of his neck with his long, narrow fingers as he shifted his head, first to the left and then to the right. She almost felt like a voyeur as she watched the play of muscles that crisscrossed his back and the rolling motion of his broad shoulders as he moved them beneath a fitted pearl-gray cotton shirt to relieve some unnamed tension.

There was an intensity about him that both intrigued and unnerved her. She was fascinated by this man and just a little bit afraid of him, although she wondered vaguely if she wasn't looking for trouble where it didn't really exist.

"It must be late," Alexa said.

Gray's fingers stilled on the tight muscles of his neck, but he didn't turn around. "Close to midnight."

"Were you still up or did I wake you?"

"I'd just come upstairs when I heard you."

"I'm sorry I disturbed you."

He turned toward her. The shadows of the room harshened his features and emphasized his fatigue. "You've disturbed me since I first set eyes on you, Alexa. I don't expect that to change."

She flinched. "Are you always so blunt?"

"Always."

Sinking back against the pillows, a small sound of distress escaped her when she shifted her leg too quickly.

"Do you need something for your knee?"

"I'd rather wait until morning."

"Martyrdom doesn't suit you."

She dismissed his sarcasm, crediting it to the exhaustion she'd already glimpsed in his face and in the tense lines of his body. She wondered if he even meant half the hardsounding things he said. "Living with the pain makes more sense than masking it. That way, I don't get a false sense of security."

"Michael likes you."

She smiled. Grayson Lennox seemed to change the subject whenever it suited him. She decided that he did most things to suit himself. "And I like Michael. He's a good boy. He talks a lot about his parents, but that's natural since he misses them so much."

"We *all* miss them."

"I know how you—"

"No," he interrupted tersely. "You *don't* know how I feel. If you did, I'm not even sure you'd understand."

Gray left the shadowed corner of the room, pausing near the end of the wide brass bed. In his mind was the haunting knowledge that death, no matter how sudden or unexpected, was never a clean break between the living and the dead. Memories lingered. Responsibilities and obligations emerged, despite any reluctance those left behind might feel.

He felt a genuine desire to dismantle the barriers he had so foolishly erected against a child who, through no fault of his own, reminded his uncle that love risked meant love lost. But he just wasn't altogether certain how to set the process in motion, although he was now convinced that with Alexa's help he could at least try.

Alexa watched him hesitate at the end of the bed. She took a deep breath, unconsciously holding it as her curiosity ran wild and she contemplated what his next move might be. He reminded her of an intricately constructed puzzle. She couldn't help thinking about what the result would be if she were given the opportunity to fit all his pieces together.

"I'll leave my bedroom door open. Call out if you need me during the night."

Surprised, Alexa simply nodded. She watched as he left the room, the sound of his booted stride fading as he made his way down the second-floor hallway.

More than an hour passed before Alexa fell back to sleep. But instead of the nightmares that had pursued and terrorized her earlier, images of an unpredictable and somewhat contrary rancher filled her dreams.

Four

―――――

Dr. Griffin arrived shortly after lunch the next day. After checking on his patient and assuring her that she was on the road to recovery, he pronounced her fit enough to begin using crutches.

Despite the fact that the doctor cautioned her against going up and down the stairs until she was stronger, Alexa was pleased by his announcement. Being confined to bed might have allowed her to catch up on some much-needed rest and consider her options for the future, but she'd grown bored with the inactivity and isolation.

Gray retrieved a pair of crutches, a memento of the leg he'd broken after being thrown from a horse a few years earlier, from a storage room in the barn after talking to Doc Griffin. As he approached the guest room, he heard Alexa and his nephew talking. He paused in the threshold of the open door, content to wait until they noticed him.

"Do you remember what we talked about yesterday, Michael?"

"Yes, ma'am."

Gray noted the less than buoyant tone of Michael's voice. Curiosity kept him quiet, but he didn't try to conceal his presence.

"I've thought long and hard about whether or not to tell your uncle about the accident," she continued, her attention on the boy's forlorn expression. "Since it won't change what's happened, and since you've already promised not to be so careless whenever you're out near the main road, I've decided that we'll keep the details between the two of us."

"Wow, Alexa—"

"But, Michael, that doesn't mean you don't share responsibility for the accident. You didn't really think when you chased after Crackers, and I panicked when I saw you run out onto the road. We're both guilty of poor judgment. If you think about it, I'll bet you'll agree with me," she said gently.

Alexa knew that she'd demonstrated extremely poor judgment herself when she'd run from the responsibility of facing her wedding guests, mountains of gifts that needed to be returned and the embarrassment she'd caused both her father and Tom.

As she watched Michael mull over her remarks, Alexa knew she'd been wrong about Lennox Ranch not being conducive to the peace of mind necessary to rethink her relationship with her father. She'd spent much of the three days since leaving Santa Barbara thinking about herself, her life and her parents.

Her late mother's diary had revealed much more than a lonely woman's emotional isolation. It had also given Alexa a glimpse of her father's disappointment at not having fathered his own child, and the betrayal he'd felt upon learning of his wife's deception.

While she regretted that her parents hadn't been able to forgive one another and work together for a happy marriage, Alexa realized that she wasn't responsible for her father's historic aloofness and disinterest in her feelings and emotional needs. She had long blamed herself for the deficiencies in their strained relationship, both as a child and as an adult. Now she knew that she wasn't responsible for her father's attitude or bewildering behavior. *He* had been wrong, because he'd punished an innocent child for someone else's mistakes.

Her greatest error had been trying to please him at her own personal expense as a means of gaining his approval. She'd done just that by not pursuing her dream of becoming a teacher and by almost marrying Tom Henderson. No longer willing to sacrifice her own dreams, Alexa still hoped to build an honest and open relationship with the man she would always think of as her father once she returned home.

She watched the boy closely, aware that he was still pondering her comments. "What do you think, Michael?"

He looked up. "I think I did a bad thing, and I won't ever do anything like that again, 'cause I know how it feels when somebody you love gets hurt or dies. You could've been hurt worser, Alexa."

She smiled at his grammar slip. "We *both* could've been very badly hurt. Just imagine what it would have been like for your Uncle Gray if something serious had happened to you."

Michael looked away before muttering, "I guess so."

Puzzled by this response from a child who appeared to idolize the man in question, Alexa drew him close and hugged him. "It might be a good idea to get a dog obedience book and teach Crackers a few basic commands."

"Minna has to go to town for groceries today. Maybe she'd drop me at the library," he said eagerly.

Gray exhaled, even more certain now that the bond of trust and friendship growing between Alexa and his nephew had the potential of benefiting all three of them.

Alexa glanced up when she heard Gray's sigh. The smile left her face as she searched his expression for some hint of what he might have overheard. She loosened her hold on Michael, her gaze darting between the two until the boy barreled out of the guest room, shouting a hurried greeting to his uncle as he raced down the hall.

Gray walked into the room, coming to a stop near the head of the bed. "Where's he off to in such a hurry?"

"The resident whirlwind decided he wanted to go to the library when Minna does the shopping."

He nodded. "Going to town usually translates into a stop for ice cream. The library isn't exactly his regular hangout."

She shrugged, determined not to tattle on the boy. It bothered her a little to go behind his uncle's back, but it came down to the fact that Michael already understood that he'd made a mistake, so there was no need to punish him further. "You know how unpredictable little boys can be."

"Not really, but it seems you do."

"I told you last night, I like Michael."

"And he likes you, but I said that last night, too, didn't I?"

She nodded, a tad uneasy with any reference to the previous night. She'd already had enough mixed messages from him and didn't feel up to dealing with any more at the moment. She glanced at the crutches. "For me?"

"Doc says you're ready for them, but they need to be adjusted. I was the last one to use them." Gray propped the crutches against the wall and reached for her. "We need to get you up on your good leg so I can see how much to lower them."

He helped her out of the bed, then carried her to a spot between the two wing chairs on the other side of the room. She stood between them, her right leg suspended above the floor. Slipping the crutches under her arms, he gauged the approximate adjustment needed.

Alexa slipped into one of the chairs while he finished his measuring, waiting tensely while he unfastened the screws and resized the crutches. "How much did you hear?" she finally asked.

Gray didn't look up from his task as he answered her. "Enough, I expect."

She tensed. "What are you planning to do?"

"I'm planning to fix these crutches for you," he said, purposely not answering her question.

"That's not what I meant, and you know it."

Gray had to work at not smiling at her edginess. "You've handled the situation. There's nothing left for me to do."

"You don't approve, do you?"

He gave her an odd look. "I approve of almost everything about you."

"But—"

"But, nothing."

She nervously tugged at the sleeve of her pale-blue peignoir, certain that Gray was playing word games with her. But why? Frustration smoldered inside her. She defensively wondered if this was just another example of male manipulation. She knew a lot about that kind of thing.

"There's something you're not saying."

"You're right. There's something I'm not saying, but I will." He extended his hand, and she complied with his silent request that she stand. "Let's see if these fit."

She accepted the crutches, settled her weight on them and then eagerly tried a turn around the room. Success would have been hers if she hadn't clipped the edge of a throw rug with the rubber-tipped end of one of the crutches. She struggled for balance, couldn't quite attain it and tumbled into Gray's arms with a startled cry.

As he caught Alexa, Gray didn't think. He simply acted on an impulse that had thrived within him for three of the longest days of his life when he looked down at her heart-shaped face. Her parted lips, wide eyes and flushed cheeks served to spur him on.

Lowering his head, he settled his mouth across her lips, felt the breathless rush of air that expressed her surprise at his behavior and savored the riotous sensation the intimate contact provoked. A muffled sound escaped her, and she tried to pull back, but Gray held her still, feasting on her lips, mounting stabbing little forays against her teeth and eventually into the soft warmth of her mouth with his tongue.

Alexa trembled and sank her fingers into his shoulders, less for balance and more for reassurance that the lightning flash skittering along her nerves was actually real and not a product of her fevered senses.

Even though he felt her response, Gray made himself release her mouth. He would have gone on, but he knew what he risked if he threw caution to the wind and indulged himself.

"I need your help with Michael."

Bewildered, she could only stare at him. Color still filled her cheeks and her breath came in ragged snatches. "Michael?"

"I need your help with Michael," he repeated, stepping away once he was certain she was steady enough to stand on her own.

"Why?"

"Will you stay?"

Already bewildered, Alexa maneuvered herself toward the bed so that she could sit down. Gray followed her, taking the crutches from her before she sank down to the edge of the mattress.

"Will you stay, Alexa?"

"Quit repeating yourself. I heard you the first time."

"Then answer me, damn it."

She glared at him and he swore again, this time so colorfully that she actually flinched at the hard sound of the words.

"Why is it so important to you that I stay?"

He ran restless fingers through his dark hair before he admitted, "I can't deal with the boy alone."

"That's crazy!" she burst out. "He adores you."

"I can't deal with him alone," he insisted.

"You aren't making any sense."

The bleakness in his eyes said there was a lot at stake here that she didn't understand, might never understand.

"My feelings about Michael aren't sensible and haven't been since his parents died. I need to work some things out where he's concerned, and you could give me the time I need. He obviously trusts and likes you. Otherwise, he wouldn't be in here at all hours of the day and night."

"You can't possibly want a stranger in the middle of personal family problems."

"You aren't a stranger."

"Of course I am."

"I don't kiss strangers."

"That was—"

"What was it, Alexa?"

"The heat of the moment," she answered.

The look he gave her absolutely sizzled. "The heat of the last three days is more like it, honey."

Once again Alexa ignored his sarcasm. "I can't believe it. You actually *asked* me to stay. You didn't order me the way you usually do."

"I must be having an off day."

"Maybe," she conceded, somehow knowing better.

"If anything happens to my parents, Michael's my responsibility. They sent him here for the summer because they know that up until now I haven't wanted to spend any time with him."

"Why on earth not?"

He looked at her, cold fury in his eyes. "I can't put it into words."

She threw up her hands in frustration. "Men! What is it with your sex? You don't talk about the things that bother you. You just slam your way through life like it's an obstacle course, ordering everyone around and rearranging things so that they suit you."

"Where the hell did that come from?" he asked, irritated because she was right.

"Don't ask."

"Fine, I won't. Can we get back to Michael now?"

"I'm not a solution for your problems with your nephew. No one person can be an answer for another person. It's nutty to even think that kind of thing will work."

"I'm not asking you to be a solution. All I need is a little time. You can give it to me."

"How?"

"By just being here."

"Nothing's that simple."

"Maybe not, but could you give it a shot?"

She sighed and rubbed her throbbing temples. She couldn't forget the struggle she'd just been through in order to come to terms with her own problems. The details weren't all worked out in her mind, but she knew now that she could go home and face the reality she'd left behind in such haste. She also admitted to herself that it would be a lot easier if she could get home under her own steam, so lingering at the ranch while she recuperated wasn't a totally insane idea.

Most of all, though, she knew that it would be up to Gray and his nephew to set things right between them. In the same way that she would have to search for common ground with her father, so would Gray and his nephew have to mend what was apparently a torn relationship.

"So what you really need is a buffer, someone who can hold her own with the two of you."

"Exactly."

"Let me think about it," she suggested, amazed that she was even considering the idea. Her personal track record hadn't exactly prepared her for this kind of tightrope walking.

"What is there to think about?" he asked impatiently. "Don't you ever do anything on impulse?"

"Too much, but not anymore. I'll give you an answer tomorrow."

He approached her and sat down beside her on the edge of the bed. He didn't miss the wary look on her face or the nervous way she laced her fingers together. As he watched her knuckles go white with tension, he said quietly, "I really *do* need your help, Alexa. I know this may be difficult for you to understand, but I think I can give Michael what he needs if I can just buy myself a little time."

Capitulation was on the tip of her tongue, so she bit it to keep from speaking. Acting on impulse with Grayson Lennox was dangerous. She'd already had ample proof of that when he'd kissed her. She'd wanted that moment to go on forever.

"Why did you kiss me?"

He looked surprised, then shook his head in wonder because it was obvious she had no idea of her own appeal or his inability to resist her. "Why does any man kiss a beautiful woman?"

"You tell me," she whispered, too curious to let embarrassment keep her from satisfying her need to know what had motivated him. When had she gone from puny to beautiful?

"I kissed you because every time I get within twenty yards of you my blood starts to boil." He laughed at her stunned expression. "I kissed you because my body's about to explode from wanting you. I kissed you because I've spent the last three sleepless nights thinking about what it would be like to make love with you until you're clawing my back and moaning my name because of the pleasure I've given you."

His words made her nerves tingle and snap, effectively touching off tiny bursts of fire in her body. Longing to feel the wildly uninhibited lovemaking he'd just described, she suddenly hated her lack of experience with men. She hated, too, that her one intimate relationship in college had ended with her deeply disappointed and wondering, "Is this all there is?"

She couldn't stop staring at him. "You shouldn't say things like that!" she exclaimed, her face flaming because she could see them together in her mind's eye.

"Why shouldn't I tell you what I'm thinking, Alexa?"

She edged away from him, moving toward the brass headboard in order to keep herself from tumbling into his arms. The realization that she would have welcomed his attention under different circumstances jolted her right down to her pale pink toenails.

"Why not?" he asked again, his voice low and his eyes narrowed as he watched her bewildered expression. He couldn't ignore the shock still flaring in her eyes. Feeling a twinge of guilt, he said softly, "Talk to me, Alexa."

"How am I supposed to trust you when you tell me you want to have sex with me?"

"Trust isn't the point. Besides, I said I wanted to make love with you, didn't I?" He reached out and pulled her gently to his side, despite a moment of resistance on her part. He could feel her trembling as he put his arm around her and drew her against his hard body.

"Yes! No! For heaven's sake! It doesn't matter how you said it, just the fact that you said it is enough."

"Having sex and making love are two distinctly different acts, Alexa." Surely she knew the difference at twenty-three. "And I've never taken a woman who didn't want me, so don't worry because I don't plan to start now."

She looked up, searching his face to be certain he spoke the truth. Momentarily satisfied but also a little disappointed that he was so easily dissuaded, though she loathed admitting it to herself, she eased out from under his encircling arm. "If I agree to stay on, it will only be because of what you've told me about the problems you're having with Michael." Her voice shook, but she made herself continue. "I won't have an affair with you."

"I don't remember saying anything about having an affair," Gray noted for the record.

"I know that, but—" Alexa broke off when he abruptly got to his feet.

He towered over her as he stood there, and she was forced to tilt her head in order to see his face. Her senses came alive again as her eyes slowly traveled up lean, hard thigh, narrow hips, a flat abdomen that she was certain had all the flexibility of a metal washboard, wide chest and even wider shoulders. She paled when she saw the disturbingly satisfied half smile on his lips.

"I won't touch you if you don't want me to, Alexa, but prepare yourself," he warned so softly that she had to strain to hear. "If you give me even the slightest hint that you're interested, all my good intentions will go up in flames, just as we will if we ever make love."

Alexa didn't see him again that day, although he might as well have camped out at the end of her bed for all the rest she got. Despite visits from the housekeeper and Michael

that should have served to distract her from her confused
thoughts, she couldn't forget what he'd said to her, nor
could she erase from her mind the intimate images his
graphic words had fostered.

Before she fell asleep late that night, Alexa finally admitted several things to herself. First, if she had any sense at all,
she would leave Lennox Ranch immediately. Grayson Lennox threatened her emotions, her newfound confidence in
herself as a woman and her determination to create a life of
substance and value for herself. She also decided she was
finished twisting herself into a pretzel in order to make other
people happy.

Conversely, she cared deeply about Michael. She also
knew how important his future relationship with his uncle
would be if Gray were ever placed in the position of assum-
ing custody of the boy. And while she knew she couldn't be
an answer for either of them, in the same way that no one
else could give her the answers to her future happiness, she
still felt that she might somehow be able to help bring them
together.

Michael had already given her a not so subtle hint of his
uncertainty about his uncle's feelings. And, to his credit,
Gray hadn't spared himself while admitting that he needed
more time to work out his own feelings about his nephew.

She didn't understand the source of his personal discord,
but she *did* care enough about him, despite the new and
frightening feelings he aroused in her, to at least try to act
as a buffer between the two while she recuperated. He had,
after all, taken her into his home when he could have just as
easily sent her on her way to a local hospital the night of the
accident. Hence, she rationalized that she owed him and
tried to ignore a conscience that reminded her that she also
wanted him.

Another part of her wondered if this situation wouldn't
also test her new resolve, sort of a dress rehearsal before she

returned to Santa Barbara. She'd already surprised herself by standing up to Gray whenever the situation called for it, something she'd never in her life felt free to do even when she'd been wronged.

Grayson Lennox was strong-willed, self-confident about everything, devastatingly blunt, wickedly attractive, overbearing, seductive to the extent that her skin ached at the mere though of his hands on her body, stubborn and so damned contrary at times that she wanted to grind her teeth in frustration. The teeth-grinding urge, however, placed a poor second to passion as she pondered what it would be like to be in his arms, senses at full tilt and mind and body no longer governed by the constraints of inexperience.

Alexa, still drowsy from a dream-ravaged night, hovered at the edge of wakefulness. Her eyes flew open and she struggled up from the bed when she heard what she immediately identified as the sound of Gray's voice raised in anger.

She flipped back the sheet and reached for her crutches, growing more alarmed as his tirade continued. When she heard, "Answer me, Michael!" she was already hurriedly making her way out of the room and down the hallway, her ears guiding her to Gray and Michael's location in the big house.

As she carefully navigated the stairs, Alexa consciously dismissed Dr. Griffin's warning that she not attempt them on her crutches until she was stronger. She finally came to a stop and paused, out of breath from her hasty descent of the staircase, in the open doorway of Gray's library.

Gray and Michael spotted her at the same moment, but their individual perspectives were uniquely different.

The man saw a disheveled beauty, her face flushed from sleep, her fair hair no longer bound in a tidy braid but tousled and cascading across her shoulders and down her back, and her satin-covered breasts still heaving from the exertion of a hurried trip down a flight of stairs.

Gray's body throbbed with aching awareness, and he drew in a sharp breath as desire fused with sudden anger. Doc Griffin had warned her to stay off the stairs, but the little idiot had ignored his instructions. It seemed everyone in his home now acted purely on impulse. Even Minna was offering opinions on subjects that didn't concern her.

The boy, on the other hand, saw an angel of mercy, an ally he knew he could trust. He relaxed visibly when she moved into the center of the room. He waited for Alexa to speak, too young to realize that she was using her slender body as a barrier between himself and his uncle.

"I could hear the two of you all the way upstairs," she said calmly, but her blue-gray eyes glittered with what could only be described as maternal outrage as she glared at Gray. She turned slowly, positioning herself so that she could look at his nephew. "What do you have to say for yourself, Michael?"

"I messed up again, 'lexa."

"Will you tell me about it?"

"I took a bucket of carrots out to the pasture for the horses, but I forgot to lock the gate when I left." He gave her a shamefaced look then glanced down at his sneakers.

"You went out to see the mares and their new foals?"

He nodded.

"Michael, what you did was serious. You've already told me that your Uncle Gray takes very special care of his horses, especially the new foals. Don't you think you owe him an apology for your thoughtlessness and a promise that you'll be very careful in the future?"

"Yes, ma'am."

He slipped out of his chair and approached Gray. "I'm sorry I made a mistake. I'll do better next time."

Too startled by what he'd just witnessed, Gray simply nodded. Michael had willingly admitted his mistake to Alexa, a stranger until four days ago, while his uncle had received only silence. But his uncle, he realized grimly, had demanded and accused. He hadn't listened. He hadn't tried to understand.

He wanted to reach out, wanted to offer reassurance and apologize for losing his temper, but he couldn't seem to find the words or the ability to utter them, even in the face of Michael's obvious sincerity. The boy turned and walked away, his narrow shoulders slumped dejectedly. Gray felt like ten kinds of a fool.

When Michael paused in the library doorway, Alexa encouraged, "Go ahead upstairs, but give some thought to what's happened this morning. We'll talk more in a little while."

He nodded and did a quick about-face. Alexa waited for his footsteps to fade before she made her way to the library doors.

Her transformation was instantaneous—from angel of mercy to avenging angel in the time that it took her to secure the library doors and pivot on her crutches so that she was facing Gray. She advanced on him, too furious to consider the consequences of anything she might say. That she might also be expressing a long-repressed reaction to the treatment she had been subjected to as a child never even occurred to her.

"How dare you?" she began in a low voice. "That child is only eight years old. He's not an adult. He doesn't think and reason like an adult. He's just reached an age where he's capable of learning how to be responsible, but you can't expect perfection. It just isn't possible."

"Alexa," Gray began, warning in his tone and in the way he held his lean, tense body. He was already angry with himself. He didn't need anyone telling him that he'd behaved like a jerk. He already knew that.

"How dare you behave so stupidly with him? And how dare you treat him so callously?" On a roll now, Alexa couldn't contain herself. "You're hurtful and destructive with him, Gray. Send him back to your parents. They must love him, despite their misguided attempt to bring the two of you together. Be honest with them and with yourself, why don't you? Tell them you hate children, since that's how you act, and be done with it. You certainly aren't the first man I've ever met to feel that way."

His expression hardened; his eyes grew cold. Lips that could be arrestingly sensual thinned. "Don't push me too hard, Alexa. You don't know what you're talking about."

She made a disgusted sound and moved nearer, abandoning any good sense she might have normally employed around him. "I wish I had a tape recorder so that you could hear yourself right now. You sound jaded and arrogant when you talk that way. Well, fine. I can deal with you, but Michael can't and shouldn't have to. He's a child, not a man, and he doesn't deserve the way you treat him. So start picking on somebody your own size."

"Just who in hell are you mad at, Alexa?" he demanded angrily, caught up in the fevered pitch of their exchange.

She sidestepped his question by asking one of her own. "Don't you see how intimidating your anger is to a child?"

"No, but you obviously do."

She stared at him.

"You do, don't you, Alexa?"

Mortified that he could read her so well, she answered honestly, "Yes, I do. You're too much like my father was when I was a child. I know all too well what it feels like to be treated with calculated disdain. It hurts, and that hurt stays in your heart for years afterward. It keeps you from reaching out and trusting people, even when you long to. It makes you afraid to trust yourself and those few people you let yourself care about, because, in the back of your mind, you know you're running the risk of having your feelings thrown back in your face.''

Gray, humbled by the truths she had just revealed and by the stark pain in her eyes, took a step closer. The astounding carelessness she'd endured as a child had obviously stayed with her. Gray realized that her past hurts now motivated her to protect Michael however she could.

He admired her strength, and he mourned the early disillusionment she'd experienced. He also understood, more clearly now than he had since the death of his sister, that Michael needed and deserved his love, not to mention his guidance and approval. Somehow, he promised himself, he would find a way to get past his own strangled emotions. Somehow, he would stop being afraid to care, stop being afraid that he would lose those who meant the most to him.

"Alexa, there's no need—"

"There's every need," she countered sharply. "Somebody's got to get through to you before you do real emotional damage to Michael. When you're a child, you don't understand that it's not necessary to succumb to the performance pressure adults impose on you. All you know when you're little is that you're willing to do anything they ask or try to be what you think they expect you to be so that they'll love you. It's an awful way to live," she choked out, furious with herself when her eyes filled with tears. She angrily dashed them away. "Please don't do that to Michael. He hasn't earned that kind of treatment from you."

Emotion charged though him like a bolt of lightning, but he kept himself under control, kept himself from offering her comfort that she would likely reject anyway. "Are you staying or not, Alexa?"

She blinked and studied his expressionless face. Renewed anger flared inside her at his terse question.

She responded impulsively. "Yes, I'm staying, even if it's only long enough to ensure that you understand how wrong you are where Michael's concerned. Right now he doesn't *owe* you his affection or respect. It's up to you to earn both. I just hope you're prepared to stop playing God and start acting like a man who has a heart."

Gray reached for her, his hands coming to rest on her shoulders despite the fact that she tried to wrench herself free. He dug his fingers into her satin-covered skin, holding her still and making her wary.

"You've got eyes that accuse, a face and a body that any woman would kill for, a tongue so sharp it could penetrate steel, skin like silk and the temper of a shrew."

"What—"

His gaze fell to the pulse throbbing at her throat, then dropped lower to her taut breasts and pebble-hard nipples. Aroused by the intensity of her emotions, they strained against the bodice of her peignoir. Gray released the air trapped in his lungs in a loud rush, effectively cutting off whatever she'd meant to say.

"In spite of all those conflicting characteristics, how is it," he mused, his voice achingly soft, "that you still remind me of the wildflowers that bring beauty and texture to the land in the first weeks of spring?"

"Why do you always say such unexpected things?" she breathed. "Are you trying to make me crazy?"

"Why shouldn't I return the favor? Because that's what you do to me, Alexa." He smiled, the change in his face inviting, seductive. He slid his fingertips across her shoulders and up the sides of her neck.

Alexa felt a jolt of awareness so strong that her knees nearly gave way. Her pulse bucked, then began to accelerate as though racing for a coveted trophy.

The heat of his fingertips was exactly as she had imagined, the anticipation she felt as he moved against her even more devastating than her fantasies. His body, now molded to hers, expressed his desire more graphically than words ever could.

Alexa shivered, struggling to repress the answering surge of awareness that made her feel appallingly light-headed. "I have to go upstairs and talk to Michael. I need to make sure he's all right."

Gray dropped his hands but didn't move away. "You're right. I'm blowing it with him, even though I don't want to. I feel like a fool."

She inched away from him, off balance again thanks to his unexpected admission and feeling more vulnerable than ever because her heart suddenly flooded with hope.

"Why don't we talk later?" she suggested. "After we've both had a chance to calm down." Was that her voice making such a calm suggestion? She didn't feel calm. She felt like the tattered edges of an old flag, one left to linger too long on a flagpole and ravaged by the elements.

Gray didn't seem to notice her retreat as he turned and wandered over to the window behind his desk. Alexa kept moving, edging closer and closer toward the library doors. She felt suffocated by emotions she couldn't control but heartened, too, by the knowledge that, if Gray was truly sincere, his relationship with his nephew could be salvaged.

Still dealing with his own feelings of failure, Gray looked up moments later to discover that he was alone in the library. He quickly rounded the side of the desk and strode out of the room.

Relieved when he saw that Alexa hadn't gotten past the second step of the staircase, he stopped her with the touch of his hand on the base of her spine. She seemed to understand his concern, pausing while he propped her crutches against the wall so that he could carry her up to her room. Gray waited until she was in bed, a light blanket arranged across her legs and lap, before he spoke.

"I'm not a cruel man, but there's a limit to what even *I* can handle. When I can, I'll tell you what's wrong. Until then, you'll have to trust me." He paused briefly when he saw her hesitant expression. He hadn't given her any reason to trust him. He knew that, and he also knew he had to try even harder not to threaten or overwhelm her. "I've turned you into a referee and that wasn't my intent. I apologize."

"I...I have a hard time with trust, too, but you've already guessed that, haven't you?" she asked quietly.

He seized the olive branch she offered. "A person can grieve a long time for relationships that fail and the loss of loved ones. Then, if you're like me, you barricade your heart and die a little bit inside every day as a result of the walls you've built around yourself. Unless, of course, someone comes along and tells you what an idiot you've become."

"Everything that counts in life seems to be a major risk. I finally realized that before I decided to leave Santa Barbara."

"Will you tell me about all that wedding business, and why you didn't want to let anyone know where you are?"

She smiled faintly, not surprised that she hadn't fooled him. "We'll trade secrets."

"I know some of yours already."

"And I know some of yours, so we're even, Gray."

"My name sounds good on your lips."

The room suddenly began to shrink in size, the walls and ceiling closing in on her.

"I still want you, Alexa. That hasn't changed, although I think maybe we both have after this morning." Even white teeth flashed as he smiled. "Stay in bed. I'll try and make peace with my nephew. I owe him that, and a hell of a lot more."

"Just let yourself love him again," she advised.

He shook his head. "If only you knew what you're asking." With that enigmatic reply, he left the room.

Alexa slumped tiredly against the pillows and closed her eyes on a wistful sigh. Grayson Lennox always managed to leave chaos in his wake. Today was no exception.

Five

As her first week at Lennox Ranch drew to an end, Alexa grew increasingly restless, despite her determination to follow Dr. Griffin's orders to the letter. The books stacked on the floor beside her bed, three or four titles that Minna brought upstairs each day for her, gave mute testimony to how she spent the majority of her time.

Releasing a heavy sigh, Alexa dropped the book she held into her lap. Not even the most scintillating novel or intriguing mystery could hold her attention any longer. More and more, her thoughts drifted to Gray. Although still somewhat wary around him, because he persisted in doing and saying the most startling things, she couldn't ignore the fact that he aroused and subtly seduced her every time he came near her.

She shivered, recalling how the touch of his fingertips when he slid his hands across her back and under her thighs so that he could carry her down to supper each night drove her to a state of nearly adolescent breathlessness. The laughter she glimpsed in his eyes told her that he knew exactly what she was feeling and why. His barely suppressed humor only served to fluster her more.

But it was the occasional unguarded moment, when his eyes and expression grew vulnerable, when she would catch him staring at her with such naked longing, that made her want to reach out to him. Still, she felt a certain pride in the fact that, so far, she'd managed to hang onto just enough sense to refrain from hurling herself at him.

She reasoned that the true source of Gray's vulnerability was his strained relationship with his nephew. Once the two closed the gap that existed between them, then their lives would go on. Trying to be an answer for Gray would be wrong. She knew, too, that allowing him to tread beyond the boundary line of simple friendship would be catastrophic for her.

With growing dismay, Alexa realized that she cared far too much for Grayson Lennox. Vowing silently to keep herself on a tight leash, she intended to continue to maintain an attitude of casual friendliness around him. She simply wasn't willing to be remembered as a partner in a meaningless affair, no matter how much she ached for a taste of his passion.

Twenty-three years of living had almost completely convinced her that everyone is essentially alone. She didn't expect that basic fact of life to change. And although she longed for a loving and mutually satisfying relationship with a man who would treat her as a lover, partner and best friend, she harbored in her heart the fear that happily-ever-after was an illusion created by dreamers, poets and lonely people.

On that less than satisfying thought, Alexa looked up to find Gray standing in the doorway of her room. She tried to

smile but couldn't. Tears unexpectedly threatened and she
swallowed convulsively.

"Why the long face?" he asked.

She shrugged, nervously pleating the top edge of the sheet
bunched at her waist. "Bored, I guess."

Gray crossed the room as she put her book aside, pushed
back the covers and moved to the edge of the bed. He noted
her flustered movements when she pushed at the long hair
that had fallen forward across her cheeks. He also saw the
faint tremor in her hands when she lowered them to her lap.

Perched on the side of the bed, Alexa didn't look up as
Gray came closer. She simply waited for him to pick her up
and carry her down to supper. It had become a ritual, one
she welcomed because she was in his arms during the time
it took him to carry her up and down the stairs. It also got
her out of the guest room at least once a day. She jumped
when he unexpectedly sat down beside her on the bed.

"Are you all right?"

"Of course."

"Want to talk about it?"

She gave him a suspicious look, then shook her head.
"I'm fine. Nothing to talk or worry about."

He frowned. Her melancholy mood and stilted replies
told him that she wasn't fine. He discarded the idea of teasing a smile from her.

Something about her posture and facial expression made
him think of Jenny. That surprised him, kept him quiet for
a moment. This was the first time he'd even thought about
his late wife since meeting Alexa.

The memory of Jenny made him smile. That surprised
him, too. Four years had passed since he'd been able to remember her and smile. With Jenny he'd experienced the
varying emotions and moods of a woman. Some of them
still bewildered him a little, and he was very rusty when it

came down to dealing with them, but at the moment he appreciated the lessons of his past.

Alexa drew in a shaky breath, then caught the clean masculine scent of the man beside her. She nearly groaned. She tried to cover her reaction by commenting, "Minna won't like her hot food cooling at an empty table."

Gray ignored her, knowing full well that his housekeeper was a good five minutes away from serving their evening meal. "Let's see what we can do to lighten your mood first."

"I don't need my mood lightened." Alexa told herself to relax. She fixed her gaze on her clasped hands and wouldn't look at him. "It's been a long time since lunch. I'd rather eat than talk."

She knew she sounded like a spoiled child, but she couldn't help herself. She felt man-haunted and housebound. Neither condition soothed her frayed nerves.

He reached out and separated her entwined fingers. Taking one of her hands, he held it in his own, absently stroking her knuckles with his callused fingertips while he waited for her to look at him. "Talk to me, honey. Tell me what's wrong, aside from a bad case of cabin fever."

She felt his touch all the way to her soul. "Don't be nice," she whispered. "You'll make me cry."

"Someone once told me that a woman needs to be moody once in a while. Is this one of those times?"

She reluctantly nodded, then risked looking up at him. She felt the breath leave her body in a soft whoosh when she saw the tenderness in his eyes. "I'm sorry. It's been a long week. I'm just not used to being so confined."

He nodded, released her hand and stood. Reaching down, he scooped her up into his arms as though she weighed no more than a thistle. He knew she hadn't told him the truth about what she was feeling, but he willingly excused her.

As Alexa rested her head against his shoulder and looped her arms around his neck, Gray wondered what had changed his spitting little cat into a trembling kitten.

Michael was already in the dining room, aimlessly prowling the area between his chair and the wall as he waited for dinner. He grinned when he saw Alexa and quickly circled around to her side of the table once Gray helped her into her chair. He clutched a collection of drooping flowers in one hand and a mason jar half filled with water in the other.

Alexa mustered a smile as she accepted the gifts, although she had to swallow against the knot in her throat that threatened to make her weep. She eased the nearly wilted collection of multihued blossoms into the wide-mouthed container.

"They're beautiful, Michael. Thank you."

Now the two of them were being patient and kind. She trembled anew, unaccustomed to such exquisite consideration. Extending her arms, she gave him a quick hug. She didn't let herself look at Gray.

Gray closed his fist around his napkin. The affection she gave so instinctively to everyone but him brought a curse of frustration to his lips. The spontaneous hugs, the reassuring smiles, the sound of her laughter, the affectionate swipe of her hand across a shoulder—he'd seen it all and wanted to share in the bounty.

He swallowed the oath still poised on the tip of his tongue. He felt little comfort in the fact that both he and his nephew instinctively connected her to the wildflowers strewn across much of the land he owned. Releasing his grip on his napkin, Gray told himself that he was a fool to be jealous of the people who lived in his home. But that didn't lessen his longing or eliminate his jealousy.

Minna saved the day. She swept into the dining room, cheerful as always, chattering about the hot weather and chickens that refused to supply her with a suitable number of eggs, and carrying a tray covered with serving dishes.

Alexa relaxed, feeling profound relief when both Michael and Gray concentrated on their food. Her appetite didn't fail her, and she enjoyed her meal, especially when she realized that she was no longer the focus of anyone's attention.

Michael supplied a running commentary on his activities with his two new friends. Gray encouraged his nephew's conversation, much to Alexa's pleasure. He appeared to be making an honest attempt at reconciliation with the boy.

She could see the difference in the two of them already. She was, however, unprepared for the little boy's question about Rivers House, although they had already talked about the orphanage and her late mother on several occasions.

"Do the kids at the orphanage get to eat together like a real family, 'lexa?"

She nodded, a smile lighting her eyes as she remembered the battle she'd waged to keep Rivers House from evolving into an institutional environment. She'd assumed control of the trust left for the orphanage at nineteen. She soon discovered, though, that many of the innovative practices established by her mother, who had founded Rivers House, had been discarded.

Alexa reinstated every one of them, added a few of her own and then promptly fired the director of the orphanage. The emotional security she had lacked after her mother's death was something she was determined to offer the abandoned children living at Rivers House.

"What's it like there?"

"We try to make it a happy and safe place, Michael," she answered, warming, as she always did, to the subject. "It's an enormous old frame house that sits on about ten acres in the foothills of Santa Barbara. My mother lived there when she was a girl, but she remodeled it so that it would be a good place for children. Every bedroom is different.''

"How?"

"Well, there's the mountain room. That one has an entire wall with skiers painted on it. Then there's the room that looks like Hawaii, with surfers and swimmers and palm trees and lots of sand. And we can't forget the doll room.''

He made a face at that. "How about a spaceship room?"

"We've got one of those, too.''

Gray listened intently, expanding his understanding of Alexa and what motivated her. Michael, however, distracted him from his thoughts.

"Wow! That'd be really neat.''

She grew serious. "It's important for you to understand that those unusual bedrooms can never make up for the families the children have lost, but they do help make them feel special. They also make them feel that they have a real home until a new family comes forward to adopt them.''

The little boy glanced at his uncle, gave him a considering look and then asked, "May I be excused?"

"No dessert?" Gray asked, alerted by the look on his face that he was seriously weighing Alexa's final remarks.

"Could I have it in the kitchen with Will and Minna?" Adding please as an afterthought, he waited for a decision.

"If they don't mind.''

Michael, on his feet and walking around the table, paused near the now closed swinging kitchen doors. "They like me, so they won't mind.''

The boy flashed a grin at Alexa and pushed into the kitchen, Minna laughter and Will's deep voice a brief burst of sound before the door swung closed again.

Gray placed his knife and fork on the edge of his plate, thoughtfully reached for his wineglass, and sat back in his chair. "He's testing me.''

"Sounds like it.''

"I guess it isn't all that surprising."

"Probably not," she agreed, pleased by his willingness to understand. "If everything I've read is accurate, he's just trying to find out where he stands with you. Then he'll decide if he's willing to accept the place you've given him in your life. He'll let you know when and what he's decided."

Gray placed his empty wineglass on the table and pushed back his chair. "How about some time in the porch swing before you go back upstairs?"

"You don't have to work tonight?"

He chuckled, aware that he'd turned into a workaholic since her arrival at the ranch. "It's Saturday. Even *I* deserve a night off once in a while."

She missed his humor. "I didn't mean to imply that you didn't."

Gray got to his feet, the movement so lithe, so powerful, so controlled and so typically him. "No offense taken, honey."

She exhaled in frustration. "Do you have to keep calling me that?"

"It suits you."

"I seem vapid and stereotypically female to you?"

"I didn't say that, now, did I?"

"You are so confusing to talk to. I never understand half the things you say to me."

"Don't you?"

"No," she whispered, flustered by his nearness when he leaned down and lifted her out of her chair. "No, I don't understand you at all," she insisted stubbornly, her heart jerking around in her body as he cradled her to his chest.

He smiled, that slow, easy smile that invariably tightened her nerves. She took a deep breath and dragged her eyes from his mouth.

"I think you understand, Alexa. You just aren't ready to admit it to yourself or to me yet."

"You're talking in circles again."

He laughed out loud. "Am I?"

He carried her out of the dining room and down the hallway to the front door, and then out to the sweeping veranda that circled the entire ground floor of the house. Within seconds Alexa was seated on the swing. Gray sat less than a foot away, his long legs stretched out in front of him and his gaze on the setting sun.

"Interesting life you have."

She glanced at him, wondering if he was making fun of her again. "As a life, it's pretty good."

"How come you're so lonely then?"

His observation had the impact of a dart striking a balloon. "Who says I'm lonely?"

"You're not lonely?"

"Of course not," she answered brightly, too brightly. "I have a busy life, people I care about, lots to do."

"You don't feel any better, do you?"

Exasperated, she turned to look at him. "Would you warn me the next time you plan to change the subject?"

"I figured I'd just keep bouncing around until I found one you liked."

"Gray!"

"Alexa!" he exclaimed, playfully mimicking her.

"Why do you always feel the need to make fun of me?" She straightened her spine, as though readying herself for a blow. "Do you dislike me that much? Besides destroying a stretch of fence, what is it exactly that I've done to offend you?"

Gray turned and pounced with absolutely no warning. He reeled her in against his body so quickly that her head began to spin. One second she was sitting as calm as could be on the porch swing. In the next, he had her in his lap and pressed intimately to his body. His mouth drew the very air from her lungs as he soundly kissed her.

There was nothing easy or gentle about him, but he didn't hurt her. She simply experienced the staggering force of desire long denied and only now set free. Had they really met just a week ago? she wondered before his intensity sucked her into a whirling vortex of pure sensation.

"How...could...I...possibly...dislike...you?" He punctuated each word with the searing pressure of his lips.

Alexa held on tight. This was what she wanted, what she'd fantasized about for hours on end during the last seven days. The reality far exceeded the fantasy.

She arched closer, then closer still, wanting to crawl beneath his skin and burrow there for the rest of her natural life. She sank her fingernails into his shoulders, mindless to the discomfort she might cause.

She heard him groan and parted her lips, allowing him entry to the heat already sparking inside her. Suddenly, he was raging fire and she was supremely combustible kindling. He scorched her flesh and her heart, made her feel feverish, frantic, out of control.

He released her as abruptly as he'd seized her. Too shattered by his rejection to understand his motive, Alexa could only stare. Her heart refused to calm and her breathing remained erratic as she watched him.

Alexa saw him throw his head back, raise his hands and press the heels of his palms to his eyes. She sensed rather than saw the tension in his long, lean limbs. She felt the heat still emanating from his powerful body. In the act of reaching out to him, she froze when she heard a car door slam shut.

She moaned softly, finally aware of why he'd stopped, but unaware of how the tortured sound she'd just made tore at him. Even in the near darkness they weren't protected, weren't shielded from the world around them. She slumped against the back of the swing, dropped shaking hands into her lap and consciously willed herself to take deep breaths.

"Alexa . . ."

"Don't say anything, please." Embarrassed by her lack of control, she longed for the privacy of the guest room.

Gray leaned forward, concern etching his taut features. He took her hands, felt the tremors shaking them. His fingers closed on the pulse points of her wrists. Worry as well as masculine satisfaction merged inside him when he grasped that she, too, was shaken by the force of what they had just shared.

"Stay put. I'll be right back."

She stared at his shadowed features. Where did he think she would go? She couldn't have moved off the swing if her life had depended on it. That inability had nothing to do with her knee, which, if the truth were known, now gave her little discomfort.

"Did you hear me?"

She nodded, then watched him stand. She listened to him draw air into his lungs, then stiffened when he paused, reached down and placed his hand on her shoulder.

"This won't take long, just a minute or two at the most." He reluctantly left her, still consciously banking the fires she had set inside him.

Alexa watched him stroll along beside the veranda railing as though he didn't have a care in the world. When he reached the front steps, the light over the double front doors silhouetted his body. She shivered and wrapped her arms around herself in spite of the sultry warmth of the summer night.

"Evening, Doc. What brings you out here so late?"

She marveled at the composure in his voice. How could he sound so unruffled? Shifting uneasily, Alexa closed her eyes and tried to gather her scattered wits while she listened to the two men talk.

"Wanted to check on our patient. I would've been here around lunchtime if Kitty James hadn't decided to have her twins three weeks early."

"Kitty's never done anything on schedule in her life. Drives her husband crazy," Gray commented with a chuckle. "Go on into the kitchen. By the look of you, you could use a cup of coffee and some of Minna's pie. I'll let Alexa know you're here."

As soon as the doctor walked into the house, Gray retraced his steps. He didn't say anything until after he carried Alexa upstairs and placed her on the bed.

Reluctant to leave her side, he watched her nervously fluff pillows and fuss with the blanket and sheet. He couldn't ignore the fact that she refused to look at him. Nor could he ignore the distress her attitude caused him.

"I must be living under a black cloud," he muttered to nobody in particular as he wore a path in the rug beside her bed.

She glanced up, finally registered his restless pacing and, very uncharitably, decided that he was like most men. He hadn't gotten what he wanted, so now he'd act like a bee-stung bear. Alexa refused to dwell on how out of sorts *she* felt.

Gray stopped his pacing and towered over her. "Say something, damn it!"

"There isn't anything to say, other than the obvious."

"Which is?" he demanded, annoyed by her brittle tone.

"Dr. Griffin did us a favor. I've already told you I won't have an affair with you."

Anger tightened his jaw and brought winter ice into his dark eyes. "How sensible and mature," he scoffed.

"Can't you just accept the fact that we both got a little carried away?"

"No, because it would be a lie. There's a lot more going on here besides sex, Alexa, so don't try and run away from me. There isn't any place to go."

"Don't you dare threaten me, Grayson Lennox," she flared defensively. "You have no right."

"Then don't lie to me or to yourself. I felt your hunger when you were in my arms, and I've had a taste of all that passion you've got locked up inside you. It's mine, Alexa, every ounce of it. I want it and you, and I'll have both."

Furious, she immediately refuted the claim he'd just staked. "You'd better think long and hard before you try and push me into a corner, Gray. I may be smaller than you, but I'll come out swinging. I don't need you or anybody else telling me how to live my life."

"Who made you so damned defensive, Alexa?"

Doc Griffin walked into the room before she could form a reply. He carried his scarred leather medical bag and a cane. The amused expression on his face assured Alexa that he'd heard their heated exchange. Gray was too angry to be embarrassed, while Alexa wanted to sink to a spot between the mattress and box springs.

"Sounds like a battle of the sexes in here," he noted conversationally. Looking at his patient, his smile broadened. "It also sounds like Grayson's finally met his match, young lady. Guess you'll be wanting this cane. Might be a good weapon if he happens to get out of line again. He's been needing somebody with a little nerve in her to brighten up his life, so don't you go running off to Santa Barbara before you have to."

Alexa nearly choked when she saw the look of disbelief on Gray's face. He stomped out of the room, his language blue enough to shock a sailor and Doc's laughter trailing behind him.

While Doc Griffin conducted a thorough examination of her knee, Alexa silently berated herself for giving in to her

fantasies. She knew better, but she'd still played a dangerous game with a very powerful man, a man capable of re-
ducing her heart to ashes if she let him.

She managed to digest the doctor's instructions despite
her inner turmoil. Two more days on crutches and then she
could start using the cane he'd propped against the night
table beside her bed.

"If you're extra careful," he advised before he left, "then
you can get around the house at your own pace while your
knee continues to heal. Don't forget to use the whirlpool.
It'll help speed up your recovery."

Minna stopped in shortly before midnight to say good-
night. Otherwise, Alexa remained undisturbed until the next
morning, when Gray carried up her breakfast tray and the
Sunday paper.

Neither one of them said a word about the previous night.
Both behaved in a scrupulously polite manner. Each seemed
determined to out-nice the other, a situation that had the
housekeeper, Will, and even Michael in stitches by the end
of the day.

Gray, stubborn to a fault, righteously decided that Alexa
should make the first move and apologize for behaving so
irrationally. Alexa expected Gray to apologize. He's started
it, she reasoned, and he should finish it.

She also kept wondering why she couldn't dismiss the incident as a simple mistake in judgment on both their parts.

By the time her second week at Lennox Ranch came to a
close, she still didn't have an answer.

Six

Exquisite. Alexa sighed contentedly, thinking how utterly exquisite it felt to be submerged in the whirlpool. She savored the serenity of these daily soaks.

The froth of bubbles lapping at her shoulders covered the entire top of the water's surface. She willingly allowed the warm moving water to lull her into a state of complete physical and mental relaxation.

Her hair, piled carelessly atop her head and held in place with two mother-of-pearl combs, responded to the room's misting heat by creating a tumbled mass of soft curls that framed her face and caressed her neck. Alexa's legs, gently pummeled by the circulating water, floated just below the surface.

She closed her eyes with another sigh. Her thick lashes formed delicate half-moons high on her heat-pinkened cheeks. A smile gently curved the edges of her mouth. Arms draped across the upper ridge of the tub, she let her hands dangle over the sides.

Gray paused at the closed door of the master-suite bathroom, aware that Alexa was inside. The gash on his forearm throbbed painfully, the result of having carelessly dragged his arm across the sharp end of a rusty nail protruding from a length of old timber stacked behind the barn.

Better him than one of his horses, he'd immediately thought, then felt like a fool because he hadn't been paying attention to what he was doing. As always, his mind was on Alexa. She would be the death of him yet. If not him, then his manhood, he thought sourly.

With Minna gone for the afternoon, Will and most of the trainers out at the oval track beyond the barn and none of the stable crew available, Gray needed help. He would have waited if he'd had another option.

Securing the towel wrapped around his arm, he rapped on the door then pushed it open. He got two steps into the room and stopped short. The subtle scent of jasmine registered in his senses a second later.

Alexa, startled by his intrusion, sat up quickly, considered the wisdom of her actions and settled, just as quickly, back into the churning water of the bubble-filled tub. She immediately noticed his torn shirt, his heat-flushed face and the blood spattered towel. "You've hurt yourself!"

"Congratulations!" he barked sarcastically, uncaring who he insulted at the moment. "Your eyes work. Guess you don't need glasses this week."

Alexa immediately grinned. She couldn't stop herself. He was still mad. She got her grin under control thanks to the scowl on his face. "Turn around," she ordered.

He didn't budge, just glared at her. Too busy trying to tamp down the havoc she inspired in his anatomy, Gray couldn't fathom her logic. "Why should I turn around? This is my bathroom."

"Because," she teased, "while I may not be Little Red Riding Hood, you're definitely my idea of a wolf." She smiled at him, more gently now. "Just indulge me this small madness," she suggested. "We'll both be glad you did."

He didn't agree, but he grudgingly did as she asked.

"Okay, you can turn around now."

He turned back to find her encased in one of his long terry robes. Despite sleeves that dwarfed her arms, despite the fact that she was at this very moment rolling the excess material up to her elbows and despite the fact that she would probably trip over the hem if she tried to walk very far, it still looked a heck of a lot better on her than it did on him. On that thought, Gray nearly growled.

"Now what?" she prodded, noticing his irritated expression. She stood there with her hands on her hips, the majority of her weight settled on her good leg, daring him with her raised chin and squared shoulders to give her any lip.

"Forget it."

He focused on the cleavage revealed by the gaping lapels of his robe, consciously fighting the urge to rip the thing right off her if she got too close. He took a shuddering breath at the thought of burying himself in her body before he turned away. She tested the tolerance of a saint, and he already knew the word didn't describe him.

"I don't need any help. I can do it myself."

Tight-lipped, he crossed the room and stood at the sink. He fiddled with the tap with his free hand, stuck his arm under the flow of water, then yelped when it came out too hot and irritated the seeping gash.

"What a baby! You would think you'd never cut yourself before." Using her cane, Alexa followed him across the sky-blue tiled floor.

He muttered something suitably nasty.

Relaxed by her long soak, she playfully cajoled, "Temper, temper!"

Against his will, Gray remembered the exact moment when he'd used those very words on her. He glared at her through narrowed eyes, tensing when she took his hand, turned it palm up, and regarded the two-inch gash above his wrist quite matter-of-factly.

"No wonder you're so crabby."

"Alexa..."

She heard the warning note in his voice but ignored it. "Are your shots up-to-date?"

"Of course."

She gave him a serious look. The slight arching of her brows prompted him to clarify, "Six months ago."

She nodded, satisfied that he was telling her the truth. She put her free hand on his elbow and nudged him a little closer to the edge of the sink. "This'll hurt, but I think you're tough enough to survive the experience."

He didn't miss the challenge in her soft voice. "Do your worst, honey, but make it snappy. I've got a ranch to run."

Alexa concentrated on Gray's arm, all the while trying to forget the man attached to it. She ran tap water, tested it until it was lukewarm, then adjusted it so that it fell softly from the faucet. After helping him out of his torn shirt, she positioned his forearm under the flow of water and tilted it to the side so that any loose debris would be flushed away.

He flinched. Alexa glanced up at him and saw him close his eyes against the pain. Her heart trembled for him, then settled down as she worked silently and efficiently.

She used medical supplies he pointed out to her in the cupboard below the sink. Once she finally applied the last strip of surgical tape to the sterile gauze covering the injury, she suggested, "You really ought to let Dr. Griffin check this. You may need stitches."

"I've had worse happen. No need to call Doc," he told her stubbornly. "He's got his hands full with *real* medical problems."

Her eyes connected with his very naked and very masculine chest as she looked up from her handiwork. She hastily glanced away, backed against the counter edge and fumbled for her cane. She bumped it with her elbow. It crashed to the floor.

Gray halted her flustered movements with his body, cornering her against the counter edge once she retrieved the cane from the floor. He held her in place with the not so subtle pressure of his hips.

She stared up at him, heat rising in her own body when she felt the hard definition of his. She didn't know what to do, couldn't imagine what to say. She wanted his touch, but she despaired that she might end up becoming something casual or meaningless in his life. She also felt fear nibble at the edge of her mind at the prospect of being overwhelmed by a man every bit as powerful as her father.

"How come you're being so nice? I certainly haven't earned that from my actions this week."

"No, you haven't," she agreed calmly, although her nerves felt anything but.

"Then why?"

She seized the first answer that popped into her head. "I'm trying to shame you into being nice back to me."

"It may work," he said half jokingly.

"I'm not holding my breath."

The pulse in his temple throbbed a primal rhythm, taunting him as he studied her. A heartbeat later, he said, "I need your hands on my body."

She shook under the impact of his whispered words. "We shouldn't."

He made a disgusted sound. "We've both been telling ourselves that for the last two weeks. I can't live in hell much longer."

She searched his face for something more than passion, something more than physical need. When she didn't find it, she looked down, her heart breaking a little.

"Alexa, put your arms around me."

She heard his whispered plea and abandoned all rational thought. Staring at his chest, she raised hands that had been clenched tightly at her sides and hesitantly placed them on the taut flesh of his belly. The muscles of his body, like velvet-covered steel, quivered and bunched at her touch.

She slowly circled his lean lower torso, sliding her fingertips all the way around until they met at the base of his spine. She experienced, on a purely sensory level, the contrasting textures of heated skin and hard muscle.

He put his arms around her. She felt the power of his body as he moved against her. She shivered, every nerve she possessed suddenly springing to life.

"Gray—" Her voice splintered, paralleling the splintering going on in her heart as she rested her forehead against his shoulder and inhaled shakily.

"Help me over to the bench."

Alarmed by the ragged sound of his voice, she jerked her head up. He'd gone frighteningly pale. A fine mist of perspiration covered his forehead and upper lip.

Alexa helped him as best she could, her cane gripped in one hand and her free arm around his waist. He managed to sink down to the bench, relieving Alexa of his weight but not the worry rushing through her.

"I'll call the Doc right away."

He grabbed her hand. "Don't. I'm all right, just thirsty. There's juice in the bar in the other room."

Alexa moved as quickly as her leg would allow. A carved oak bar and two leather chairs, positioned in an alcove on the far side of the bedroom, were easy to find. So was the juice. She returned to Gray in less than two minutes.

She stood between his sprawled legs. He had his head against the wall, his eyes closed. The shallowness of his breathing was evident in the rapid rise and fall of his broad chest. Color slowly came back into his face, but not quickly enough to eliminate the concern Alexa felt.

He opened his eyes. "Stupid, isn't it? I hate the sight of my own blood. I can handle other people or the horses when there's an emergency, but I can't stand the sight of my own."

She decided not to say anything, although she didn't find his behavior stupid, just very human. She felt oddly comforted by this confirmation of his vulnerability.

Alexa handed him the juice, remained positioned between his knees with the aid of her cane and watched to make sure he drank it all. After he drained the glass, she took it and placed it between two potted Boston ferns that had been arranged on a tiled ledge above his head.

"If you're not feeling any better, I can still call the doctor," she offered.

"No need. I'll be all right in a couple of minutes." He patted the bench cushion. "Sit with me."

She gladly did as he asked, more because she wanted a chance to share a few peaceful moments with him than because she felt any physical discomfort as a result of standing.

Again, Gray leaned his head back against the wall and closed his eyes. He silently savored the concern that Alexa had just shown him. She was an instinctive nurturer, despite her skittish ways and blowtorch of a temper.

Her temper still surprised him. To look at her, he would never have expected her to be so defensive. It made him wonder why. He took her hand and laced their fingers together. Pleasure surged through him when she didn't pull away.

```
***********************************************************
*  You may have already won a lifetime of cash payments *
*  totaling up to $1,000,000.00!  Play our Sweepstakes  *
*  Game--Here's how it works...                         *
***********************************************************
```

Each of the first three tickets has a unique Sweepstakes number.
If your Sweepstakes numbers match any of the winning numbers
selected by our computer, you could win the amount shown under
the gold rub-off on that ticket.

Using an eraser, rub off the gold boxes on tickets #1-3 to
reveal how much each ticket could be worth if it is a winning
ticket. You must return the <u>entire</u> card to be eligible. (See
official rules in the back of this book for details.)

At the same time you play your tickets for big cash prizes,
Silhouette also invites you to participate in a special trial of
our Reader Service by accepting one or more FREE book(s) from
Silhouette Desire.® To request your free book(s), just rub off
the gold box on ticket #4 to reveal how many free book(s) you
will receive.

When you receive your free book(s), we hope you'll enjoy them
and want to see more. So unless we hear from you, every month
we'll send you 6 additional Silhouette Desire® novels. Each book
is yours to keep for only $2.24* each--26¢ less per book than
the cover price! There are <u>no</u> additional charges for shipping
and handling and of course, you may cancel Reader Service
privileges at any time by marking "cancel" on your shipping
statement or returning an unopened shipment of books to us at
our expense. Either way your shipments will stop. You'll
receive no more books; you'll have no further obligation.

Plus—you get a FREE MYSTERY GIFT!

If you return your game card with <u>**all four gold boxes**</u> rubbed
off, you will also receive a FREE Mystery Gift. It's your
immediate reward for sampling your free book(s), **and** it's yours
to keep no matter what you decide.

P.S.

Remember, the first set of one or more book(s) is FREE. So rub
off the gold box on ticket #4 and return the entire sheet of
tickets today!

*Terms and prices subject to change without notice.
 Sales taxes applicable in New York and Iowa.

"Talk to me, why don't you? Tell me why you left Santa Barbara and why you don't want anyone to know where you are."

She silently lauded him for not pressing her on this issue in the two weeks since her arrival at the ranch. She no longer felt devastated by the truth and didn't mind sharing it with him.

"A few hours before my wedding," she began quietly, "I discovered that my father wasn't my real father. He married my mother because he believed she was pregnant with his child, but she confessed the truth to him before I was born. If her diary's accurate, they started out as friends, but they wound up living their own personal version of hell."

"That must've been a shock, but it still doesn't explain why you walked out on your wedding."

"In a way, it does. My mother died when I was twelve. I'm an only child, but I've never had a very good relationship with my father. In fact, I've spent most of my life trying to get him to notice me and give me his approval. I thought if I did everything he expected of me, then maybe he'd give me his love."

He forced air through his front teeth in a tuneless whistle. "No wonder you understand Michael's feelings so well."

"*You* love Michael." Alexa smiled somewhat sadly. "Although I can't honestly say that my father doesn't love me, I don't think he's ever forgiven me for being another man's child. I don't really know how he feels," she confessed honestly. "But I *do* know what it was like to be twelve years old, suddenly without a mother and with no one to turn to. He wouldn't talk about her, wouldn't even allow her name to be mentioned in conversation."

"Sounds like a hard man," Gray commented in a subdued voice, wondering if he'd been that hard on his nephew.

"He can be," she admitted, although it still bothered her to characterize her father so negatively. "To make a long story short, after reading my mother's diary a few hours before the ceremony, and after getting all decked out in my wedding finery, I arrived at the church and realized that I was about to do exactly what she'd done.''

"Get married because you're pregnant?" Gray asked, obviously startled.

"Hardly," she replied, her tone abrupt. "The similarity was that I was about to marry a man I didn't love. Part of my motivation for getting married stemmed from the fact that my father approved of Tom." She didn't mention that she'd longed for a home and family of her own, expecting that those two things could somehow replace the love she now knew she needed in order to feel complete. "He's being groomed as the next president of Rivers International. Anyway, Tom helped me leave before anyone realized what was going on."

"No one?"

"I wasn't ready to face my father or four hundred wedding guests. I know I blew it. I should have faced up to my responsibilities then and there."

"Don't be so hard on yourself. You'd had a shock."

She shook her head. "That's no excuse for rudeness."

Gray didn't waste time arguing with her. "What are your plans?"

"Finish getting well, go home, face my father with the truth and see if we can work something out," she itemized, "return over two hundred wedding gifts and then get on with my life."

She made it sound simple, but he knew it wouldn't be. Repairing a life was never easy. "You're sure you don't want things back the way they were? It might be easier."

"Absolutely not."

He saw the glint of determination in her eyes and smiled.

Looking at her hands, Alexa didn't notice his approval. "I studied to be a teacher. That's what I'm going to do, with or without anyone's permission," she said fiercely.

"I believe you."

She flushed. "Sorry, but this is all pretty new right now. I still have some adjusting to do while I finish revamping my life and my self-image."

"You seem to be holding your own," he observed wryly.

"Maybe." She couldn't stop thinking about the phone call she needed to make.

"Does anyone know where you are?"

Alexa wasn't surprised that he still wanted the answer to his second question. "No one, but that'll change soon."

"You're going to call home?"

She nodded. "I've delayed too long as it is."

"Maybe, maybe not," he said quietly, his facial expression unrevealing. He glanced at her and was surprised by what he saw in her eyes. "You're nervous, aren't you?"

"Very."

"You can't be afraid of much, not with that temper of yours."

I'm afraid of being hurt, she almost said out loud. Instead, she sheepishly admitted, "The temper's something I've just discovered in myself."

"Are you trying to tell me I bring out the shrew in you?"

"No." She sighed. "But I *do* think being here has helped me find the person who's been hiding inside me, the same person who's spent nearly twenty-four years trying to please everyone at her own expense. Sounds pretty pathetic, doesn't it?"

"No," he said thoughtfully. "Just very sad and very lonely."

Alexa lapsed into silence. Content to sit there with Gray, she leaned her head against the wall in a pose that matched his. Eventually, though, she gave in to a random urge and asked, "What are you thinking about?"

He looked surprised, but responded anyway. "My wife, Jenny."

Alexa jerked upright. "You're married?"

"I was. She died four years ago."

She sank against the wall. "I'm sorry."

"Me, too," he answered simply, his defenses somewhat askew. "She had an inoperable brain tumor. It seemed like one day we were happy and the next day she was dead. She started having headaches. After a few weeks, she decided to see Doc Griffin. He sent her to several specialists in Sacramento and San Francisco. She didn't last a month. I spent a lot of time looking for someone to blame after she died. It took me a while to understand that what happened wasn't really anyone's fault."

"That's part of grieving, I think. I know it was that way for me. I was furious with my mother when she died. I thought she'd abandoned me on purpose. After that, I was mad at the whole world. It took me a couple of years to work it all out."

"I loved Jenny more than life itself, but that didn't keep her alive."

Gray stood abruptly, angry with himself for verbally foraging through his past, a past that reflected more pain than he was willing to rehash with anyone, even Alexa. He cared too much for her already, and he didn't want the risks attached to the feelings.

Sharing meant caring. Caring was only a heartbeat away from loving, especially when someone like Alexa was involved. And, if he let himself love her, then he would surely lose her. He knew that bitter fact of life better than he knew his own name.

"And then your sister and brother-in-law died last summer," she whispered when he paused in the doorway. "How awful for you."

Gray tried to protect them both with his next remark. "I don't want or need your pity," he said harshly.

And you'll be damned before you let anyone love you, she silently finished for him.

Despite her turbulent thoughts, despite the tears of frustration sliding down her cheeks and despite the urge to try, Alexa knew she could never compete with the perfect memory of a dead woman.

Gray walked out of the barn that housed his office and into the brilliant late-morning sunshine. Raising his arms, he stretched the kinks from his broad back and powerful shoulders. The stiffness resulted from the hours he'd spent since dawn attending to the paperwork generated by one of the most successful horse farms in the country.

As he lowered his arms to his sides, Gray thought about the horse owners who now routinely availed themselves of the full-service thoroughbred facilities of Lennox Ranch. Whether boarding brood mares, breeding, foaling out select brood mares, breaking and training young horses or providing lay-up space during the off-season, the picture-book environment of the ranch reflected the high standards and quality care his clients required and consistently received.

He'd begun with little more than a dream, a burned-out farmhouse and fifteen hundred neglected acres nearly ten years ago. He'd committed his life, all his investment capital and his talent and instincts for the horses themselves and built the ranch to its present status. Now he was a force to be reckoned with in the exclusive equine world.

While more than satisfied with his professional achievements, a sense of incompleteness had begun to gnaw at him.

Jenny's death had nearly destroyed him. He'd finally gotten past his rage and his hurt, but he'd learned a painful lesson in the process. He believed that he was better off on his own. Meeting Alexa made him want more, though. He longed to open himself to her, but he was afraid to get too close, afraid to need her too much.

She was as different from Jenny as any woman could be, but that was good, he reasoned. It was Alexa who had captured his heart with her headstrong nature, her compassion and her big blue-gray eyes, not any similarity to a woman now consigned to his memories.

Yes, he admitted to himself, he wanted her, the consequences be damned. Still, he hesitated. Was a chance at happiness worth the risk? Could he jeopardize his emotions and his sanity one more time? Would he survive the experience if the past repeated itself?

Gray exhaled heavily then glanced up when he heard footsteps on the asphalt path leading to the barn. Spotting Alexa, he drew in a sharp breath. His body stilled and his lungs burned with suppressed air.

Clad in cuffed khaki shorts, a matching sleeveless top and leather huaraches, she stood poised at the edge of one of the walkways that linked various buildings and holding pens to the ranch's racetrack. With her body angled forward, she rested her weight against her cane and watched the activity in the corral. Long fair hair, swept off her face with gold combs, tumbled across her shoulders and down her back.

He stepped back into the shadowed doorway of the barn. He didn't think Alexa knew he was there. Her attention was on Lucky Streak, his prize stallion. An animal with excellent lineage and the winner of more than two dozen races in his noteworthy career, he now stood at stud, along with two other stallions Gray owned, at the ranch during the breeding season.

As he watched her slowly make her way down the path that ran like a black ribbon around the holding pen, Gray couldn't deny that he'd deliberately avoided her during the past four days. His behavior bordered on ludicrous. He knew it, but he rationalized his actions by telling himself he was doing them both a favor by staying away from her. They either dueled verbally or struggled with the scorching desire that constantly flared between them. Either way, the situation between them had become volatile.

Sleeping on the couch in his office, when he managed to chase her image from his mind so that he *could* sleep, and eating after normal meal hours, when he had an appetite, kept him alive. He repeatedly told himself that he would survive. His nephew needed her, so his feelings had to remain secondary. He could get back to normal once she left.

Gray swore, startling the stable boy cleaning out a nearby stall. Normal! His life would never be normal again. He knew he was a fool to even think it might settle back into what had been a satisfactory, albeit somewhat routine, life prior to Alexa.

He knew he was making progress with Michael. But the boy would suffer if she left too soon. His nephew clearly loved her, willingly expressing his affection with an honesty that shamed his uncle.

Love. The word assaulted his senses like a blow from an assailant.

Love. He didn't want anything to do with the emotion, but he craved Alexa's tenderness, her passion and anything else she might willingly give.

Gray abandoned his thoughts and refocused on his houseguest. She'd prospered during her time at the ranch. The circles under her eyes were gone, as was the gauntness he'd seen in her features the first time he'd really looked at her. The nasty bruising from the torn ligaments around her knee had begun to fade, too, leaving long, golden limbs for his eyes to caress.

He clenched his fists, his body aching almost painfully as she moved toward him. She had the legs of a dancer and the body of a centerfold. He sensed that she wasn't really aware of her womanliness. Hence, she didn't try to conceal or even emphasize the curves and hollows nature had so generously provided.

Gray shifted uncomfortably, aware of the growing snugness of his jeans. Every time he got near her, he wanted her. Annoyed with Alexa and angry with himself, he walked out into the sunlight, his jaw noticeably tight and his dark eyes snapping a challenge. He stopped abruptly when he heard Will call out to him.

"Boss? We got a little problem in here."

Gray frowned. Will didn't have *problems*. He turned and retraced his steps, stopping at an open door located at the end of the passageway that separated his office from the stalls of several horses. He heard Alexa's uneven tread behind him, but he didn't turn around. The condition of the tack room and the guilty faces of Michael and the two Wilcox boys held his attention.

Alexa could tell by the set of his shoulders and the grim line of his mouth that Gray was in a snit about something. As she carefully made her way down the freshly washed cement center aisle of the stable, she said a silent prayer, hoping that Michael wasn't the object of his displeasure. The two had managed to forge a truce between them. She didn't want anything to ruin it now.

"Michael, get out here right now and bring your buddies with you."

"Yes, sir."

The three trooped out of the tack room. They looked guilty and resigned to punishment. Michael looked the most resigned, but then he lived at the ranch.

Alexa didn't say anything. One glance at the tack room told her much more than she needed to know. A second glance at Will's face, which was normally wreathed in a smile, and she redefined grim.

She crossed her fingers, praying that Gray wouldn't lose his temper and thoughtlessly embarrass Michael in front of his friends. No child, whatever his crime, deserved that kind of treatment. But given Gray's moodiness in recent days, she didn't hold out much hope of him staying in control. She sighed softly, but didn't move away.

Gray heard her soft exhalation. Instinct made him want to turn to her, made him want to understand the strangely sad sound. Instead, he focused on the three boys standing tensely in front of him.

"You three know what you've done, don't you?" he asked after several deliberately silent minutes of eye contact.

"Yes, sir," they answered in unison.

"Why?"

"We thought we'd make a fort," Michael admitted.

"You three know how to muck out a dirty stall?"

"Yes, sir." They all but groaned.

Alexa hid a smile behind her hand, realizing they'd just been sentenced to the dirtiest job at the ranch.

"Good. I'll expect each of you to show up every morning for the next week at seven sharp. Don't be late."

"What about Sunday, sir?" the younger of the Wilcox boys asked nervously. His expression said the Lord was much more intimidating than Grayson Lennox. Alexa had her doubts.

"Be here directly after church. If you don't show up, I'll call you mom to ask why." He gave them each a hard look. "Understand?"

"Yes, sir," they chorused in perfect unison.

"Playtime's over for the rest of the day, boys. Say your goodbyes. Ask Minna to drive your friends home, Michael."

Michael nodded and hustled his two friends out of the barn. Their hasty exit rivaled the most recently documented land speed record.

Gray looked at Alexa. Her broad smile shocked him, then sent pleasure skittering down his spine. By the look on her face, he'd finally done something right.

Will glanced at the two of them before nodding to himself. "I'll tend to my tack room, boss. Those kids couldn't undo the mess they just made in a month of Sundays."

"Fine," he answered, only half aware of Will as the older man stepped away.

"He certainly got your attention, didn't he?"

Gray frowned, a little taken aback by her question.

"That's what he wants, you know. This could have been a bid for it."

He ran his hand across his face, considering her remark. "I don't think so. Doing something like that usually isn't a premeditated act. They were having fun and were thoughtless in the bargain."

Alexa didn't think so. "Maybe, maybe not. I hate to say this, but Michael might have orchestrated the fort idea."

He gave her a doubtful look.

"As I said, he wants your attention. Positive or negative. He's at a stage where he'll settle for whatever he can get. I've seen it happen before."

"What were you grinning at before?"

"You," she answered, guileless in her honesty.

"I'm funny?" he demanded hotly, his well-concealed temper finally evident.

"I was proud of you. You could've ripped into him and no one would have blamed you. Will's going to spend hours putting that room back together. It shouldn't have happened."

He clenched his fists in frustration. "You don't think very highly of me, do you?"

"Of course I do! I also think you're a man who cares very deeply about a little boy who's extremely vulnerable right now, despite the progress he's made in adjusting to the deaths of his mother and father." She reached out, briefly touching his arm. "This is hard for both of you. I know that, but what you did today was wonderful."

"I was close," he admitted, relaxing a bit. "Damn close."

"I know," she said softly. "That's why I was proud of you." She shifted nervously under his steady, narrow-eyed gaze. "I need to get back to the house. I'm expecting a call from Santa Barbara in a little while."

"Your father?"

Alexa nodded and carefully started to turn around. Gray stopped her with the touch of his hand on her shoulder. She glanced at him, twisting slightly and using her cane for balance.

"Still nervous?"

"A little, but not as much as before. I tried to call him earlier in the week, but apparently he's been on a business trip to Europe."

"I'll walk up to the house with you."

"Thanks."

He shortened his normally long-legged stride to match her slower pace. "How's your knee?"

She glanced up at him, wondering if he was in a hurry to have her gone, out of his life once and for all. She also wondered what he would say if he ever learned how much she dreaded the prospect of never seeing him again, or what he would do if he discovered how she felt about him.

"Getting a little better every day," she answered, striving for a light tone.

The phone rang as they walked into the kitchen a few minutes later. Gray answered it and told the caller to hold on.

To Alexa, he said, "It's for you, your father's secretary. Use my library. You won't be disturbed in there."

She nodded and made her way down the hallway, her knuckles white against the dark mahogany handle of her cane. Gray found her in the library ten minutes later, the phone still cradled between her ear and shoulder. She didn't look up when he paused in the doorway.

"Embarrassing you was the last thing on my mind, but you're right, Father. I *am* responsible for all my actions, past and present, good or bad. Please thank your housekeeper for packing up the wedding gifts. Once I'm home, I'll send notes to everyone."

She paused briefly, then commented, "I agree. We need to talk, but not on the phone. We need to be face-to-face, and we both have to be honest with one another. When I know my plans, I'll call you, but until then you're going to have to accept that I know what's best for me now."

She carefully replaced the receiver after saying goodbye and slumped back in the chair. She didn't notice Gray as she pressed her fingertips to her forehead and massaged her throbbing temples.

He sat down across from her, his expression compassionate. "Rough?"

She lowered her hands and shook her head. "Not nearly as bad as I expected. I don't think he's ever been so subdued before. He actually *listened*. That surprised me a little, I guess. He's not usually so...cooperative."

"Maybe your leaving shook him up a little. You're his only child, after all. Maybe he cares a lot more than you think."

She studied him, optimism flaring briefly in her eyes at his words. "I don't want to get my hopes up, but it would be nice if things turned out that way."

Gray heard the wistfulness in her voice. It corresponded with the tightening in his chest that occurred every time she mentioned leaving the ranch.

"How about lunch and then a tour of the ranch?"

"I can't risk riding yet."

He lifted his eyebrows in surprise. "You know how to ride?"

"Just the basics. I took riding lessons for a short time when I was little."

"If you know the front end from the back end, you're doing better than most of the world." He got to his feet. "We can still take the tour, if you're interested. We'll use the Jeep."

She grinned spontaneously. "I'd love it. The view from the balcony is great, but I'd enjoy a closer look."

Gray silently applauded himself for distracting her from the phone call and bringing the light back into her eyes.

"Are you hungry?" he asked.

She stood with a little assist from her cane. "Starved. I'm totally hooked on Minna's cooking."

He smiled down at her, and they walked out of the library. For once, Gray was glad that Minna and Michael were out of the house, if only for a short while.

"I've decided you might be right," he announced while they ate their sandwiches at the kitchen table.

Alexa reached for her glass of iced tea. "About what?"

"What you said about Michael earlier. If he's still testing me, whether consciously or subconsciously, then that might mean he's bored, too. I'm going to put him to work on a regular basis, with an allowance. My dad did that with me when I was his age. It might help him feel more secure."

"He loves the horses, Gray. I can't imagine him turning you down."

He pushed aside his empty plate and reached for a brownie from the platter in the center of the table. "His parents were ranchers, but you probably already know that."

She nodded but didn't stop eating.

"Maybe having him out in the stables will help us find the common ground we need," he mused.

"All you can do is try," she answered softly, unaware that her eyes were filled with a mingling of emotions that shook Gray to his very soul.

He was experienced enough to recognize a woman's admiration, so he knew the look, but it had been a long time since love, admiration and respect had been combined in such a captivating package. Without being aware of it, he immediately reverted to his hard-nosed-rancher pose, his instinctive shield against feeling anything other than manageable emotions for anyone he cared deeply about.

"I'll be back in ten minutes. Be ready."

The kitchen door slammed. In midchew, Alexa shook her head in disbelief. She nearly choked on her tuna-fish sandwich as she struggled not to laugh.

She, too, was experienced, experienced enough to ignore the bite of Gray's words, experienced enough with him to know that he was running from something. Had she somehow managed to upset his well-ordered existence just a little bit?

Alexa quickly sobered. Playing games with a man like Grayson Lennox had already proven to be a dangerous pastime. The rules were his, and he changed them to suit his needs. So, no matter what she did, no matter how clever she might be, she still couldn't win.

Seven

Gray knew it was a mistake.

He knew it as he drove the final half mile to the top of the rise, parked the Jeep in a natural culvert carved out by heavy spring rains and turned off the engine. Still, he couldn't seem to stop himself. Feigning relaxation, he leaned back comfortably, propped a booted foot on the battered dashboard and slid his arm across the back of Alexa's seat.

He focused on the horizon, the brim of his Stetson pulled low across his forehead like a visor that could protect him from the prying eyes of the world. He felt vulnerable, his soul naked, his innermost feelings suddenly exposed.

He also felt like a fool. He hadn't thought about sharing this part of the ranch with Alexa. Instead, he'd just done it. Impulsively and thoughtlessly, like an adolescent out to impress his first girl.

Alexa could only stare. Words seemed inappropriate, so she didn't even try to speak. After a guided tour of the extensive and meticulously maintained thoroughbred ranch, she hadn't expected to see anything even more remarkable. But this seemingly limitless expanse of untouched acreage gave eloquent testimony to the less visible side of a man who preferred to present himself to the world as hard and tough.

Wildflowers, like a multicolored cape draped across the land, stretched all the way to the horizon. The diversity of color amazed her. The sight took her breath away, even made tears throb unreleased in her throat.

Gray remained silent, despite Alexa's obvious surprise and pleasure. This was his private place. Whether to celebrate, to mourn or to think, this was the space he occupied. He'd never brought anyone here, not even Jenny. He'd needed the beauty and the solitude for himself, a spot that was his and his alone. Correction. He had until now.

Gray opened his clenched fist just as Alexa leaned back against her seat. Her long hair, tumbling across her shoulders and over the top edge of the seat, tangled in his fingers.

His memory, he realized, hadn't failed him. The texture of her hair still reminded him of silk. He wound a long strand around his wrist, thinking that he might as well be bound to her with silken chains. The thought was whimsical and totally out of character.

Startled, Alexa glanced at him. She didn't know what to make of the expression on his face. She couldn't be sure if it reflected pain or pleasure, nor did she understand the significance of either emotion.

Gray withdrew his wrist from the silken bond and trailed his fingers up the side of her neck. She held her breath as he eased them into her hair and pressed them to her warm scalp. Her eyes fluttered closed, her breath escaping in a sudden rush from her body when he curved his entire hand to conform to the shape of her head.

Fascinated by her response to his touch, Gray watched her features as he leaned closer. A hint of color fanned her face and gave added definition to already elegant cheekbones. Her delicate eyelids trembled. Air sighed in and out of her body at a rapidly increasing pace.

He moved nearer, every inch an agony of restraint. He didn't want to overwhelm her. Hell! He didn't want to be overwhelmed by her, either.

Gray slid his hand lower. His fingertips danced lightly across the back of her neck, moving gently across the fine hairs at her nape. He felt the soft shudder that went through her body and welcomed the answering tremors that consequently surged through his own.

Although nearly torn apart by desire, he held very still. Alexa opened her eyes and looked at him, a silent query in the blue-gray pools. She started to speak. He shook his head. She nervously moistened her lips with the tip of her tongue, a classically provocative female gesture that elicited a classically male response.

Gray released a rumbling groan and gathered her into his arms. He stopped fighting himself. He simply gave in to the need and hunger that had driven him nonstop for two and a half weeks.

Alexa moaned. She lifted her arms and looped them around his neck, as hungry and need-filled as Gray.

He felt it the instant she began to break apart in his embrace. It was almost as though some barrier had shattered inside her. A matching barrier, one even stronger and more fortified, splintered and started to collapse inside him.

He savored the bite of her fingernails through his shirt as she clung to him. He delighted in her spontaneity when she parted her lips for his tongue, matching him stroke for stroke until he thought he would fragment like exploding glass if he couldn't have more of her.

She didn't resist when he ran his hands up under her loose top. She couldn't have even if she'd wanted to. His fingertips, calloused from years of hard work, smoothed along her back and waist, leaving a trail of tiny fire bursts.

She shuddered, pressing herself into his hands when he brought them up to caress her breasts. Even through her delicate lace bra, she could feel the heat and tension of his touch. Relief flooded her when he released the front clasp.

She filled his hands, her erect nipples and firm breasts enticing treasures. Gray knew that the gifts she offered should be cherished, and he was just rational enough to understand that the confined interior of the Jeep was hardly the place for lovemaking, especially not their first time.

He wanted to go slowly with her. He wanted to take the time that Alexa deserved. And he wanted her to know how dearly he valued her.

He felt one of her hands fall to a spot on his thigh above his knee. At first he thought she was simply steadying herself. Whatever her motivation, the rhythmic kneading of her fingertips soon had his muscles tensing in reply to her evocative touch.

Sanity finally pierced the seductive haze enveloping him. His body resisted, but Gray made himself pause. He reluctantly lifted his mouth from her lips and stared down at her. "My God, Alexa! There's so much fire in you."

She blinked and looked away, her eyes enormous, her lips parted and damp from the hungry stroking of his tongue. Stunned, she sank back against the seat, arms folded protectively across her breasts. She trembled visibly, still caught in the heady sensations assaulting her body.

Alexa risked a glance, nearly cringing when she saw that Gray's expression had changed from desire to apparent regret. Anticipating his next comment, she made herself speak first. The words emerged in a ravaged whisper. "That shouldn't have happened."

He yanked his hat from his head and roughly ran his fingers through his dark hair. He felt her eyes on him, wary and watchful. "It's happened before, and it'll probably happen again."

"No!"

He glared at her, his dark eyes nearly incinerating her. "Why not?"

"I won't be used, especially not by you."

"Used?" he all but bellowed. He finally saw the uncertainty and distrust in her expression. "I don't want to use you, Alexa. I may want to make love with you, but I damn well didn't bring you up here to take advantage of you."

"Then why?"

"I've never brought anyone up here before," he told her, not really answering her question.

He didn't have the courage to admit that every time he thought of her, he also thought about the wildflowers. She had become a part of his mental landscape, just as the undisturbed acres of wildflowers were a part of the landscape of Lennox Ranch.

"I don't understand."

"Don't feel alone," he muttered, his tone sarcastic thanks to his frustration with himself and the way he'd handled the situation. "Alexa, can't you try and trust me just a little?"

"You keep asking me to trust you, but so far you haven't given me one solid reason why I should. I don't understand you, and I don't understand what you want from me, aside from the obvious."

She stubbornly ignored the shocked voice in her head that told her she ought to quit kidding herself. She *did* know that he was trustworthy, just as she knew what they both wanted.

"I don't want sex from you! If that was all I wanted, I could get it anywhere." He slammed his hand against the steering wheel, unaware of just how revealing his last comment had been. "It isn't sex," he insisted earnestly. "Look,

I'm just as rattled as you, but believe me, what's going on here is something other than sex, something a whole lot more important. If you'd stop lumping me in with all the other people who've obviously taken advantage of you in the past, maybe you'd understand that.''

Hurt, Alexa turned toward the door and refastened her bra. Gray saw the self-protective gesture and nearly reached out, but something about the rigid way in which she held herself warned him to leave her alone for now.

Conversation would be pointless, too. All the words in the world wouldn't solve their current problem, and neither one of them seemed able to remain levelheaded. Gray swore, something he found himself doing more and more lately.

''Take me home, please.''

He nodded brusquely and turned the key in the ignition, still too angry to pick up on the significance of Alexa's slip of the tongue.

Twenty silent and utterly unnerving minutes later, Alexa scrambled out of the Jeep, nearly falling in her haste to be alone. Gray caught her before she could land on her nose, but she jerked free of him and limped up the flagstone path to the kitchen with the aid of her cane.

Alexa remained upstairs throughout the rest of the day and into the evening. She convinced a worried Minna that all she needed was quiet time and a project of some kind to occupy her idle hands. She didn't say anything to her about Gray, although by the look on the older woman's face, Alexa suspected she didn't have to.

In the same low-key way that she had already begun to incorporate Alexa into the workings of the household, whether by soliciting her opinions on meal planning or advice on matters concerning Michael, the housekeeper gave her a stack of mending to keep her busy. She judiciously kept her opinions to herself about her employer's erratic behavior since Alexa's arrival at the ranch.

Embarrassed by what had happened with Gray, Alexa didn't feel ready to face him. Something crucial had changed between them, but she was hard-pressed to label it. She told herself that she would be more clearheaded in the morning, although she truly doubted that she would ever be clearheaded where Gray Lennox was concerned. Her conscience told her that she was hiding from herself and Gray, but she ignored the niggling little voice. She couldn't deal with it now.

Gray, however, didn't see any reason to leave Alexa alone indefinitely. He wanted the smile back on her face and decided he would do most anything to get it there. He'd already figured out that she was struggling to be free of her past. Alexa was also fighting for her own identity, which amazed Gray. She didn't seem to realize how unique and special she was, or the difference she'd already made in the lives of the people she touched. Her gentleness, her compassion, even her sunny smile, had already changed everyone at the ranch.

If she thought she wasn't needed, then she might leave. That potential reality worried him the most. He knew it was up to him to help Alexa feel contented and busy, not to mention available to his nephew, who benefited daily from her presence.

Gray ignored the fact that she'd also touched his heart, rationalizing that much of the harmony and laughter she'd brought into his life and his home would have eventually occurred anyway. The rationalization didn't hold water for more than five seconds, but he pushed his awareness of his flimsy rationale to the back corner of his mind to avoid dealing with it.

Gray realized that at the moment, his major challenge was convincing Alexa of her value to the ranch.

With that thought in the forefront of his mind, Gray ate his first meal in the dining room in four days—alone. Although he knew by the look on her face that Minna would have happily pointed it out to him had he asked, he didn't miss the irony of the situation.

While he sipped his after-dinner coffee, he gave serious thought to Alexa's protest that she wouldn't be used. Already armed with considerable knowledge about her background, it didn't surprise him that she didn't trust him. She obviously felt manipulated and managed. She also seemed determined to fight anyone who tried those tactics on her ever again.

When his conscience kicked, Gray thought long and hard about his own motivation. He didn't want to control Alexa; he simply wanted to give her a reason to find pleasure at the ranch, a way to feel useful and necessary, which she already was.

The solution came to him the minute he walked into the downstairs library and noticed the stack of sample books left by an interior decorator hired to furnish the recently built guest cottages at the ranch. Constructed to house visiting horse owners when they brought their mares for breeding, the four cottages needed a woman's touch.

Alexa was just that woman. She had a personal sense of style he admired, and she'd spent her life moving in the wealthy circles inhabited by many of his clients. This job, one he secretly dreaded doing himself and had put off for several weeks now, might also give her a sense of her own worth.

He strolled into her room a few minutes later. "You're bored to tears sitting around here waiting for your knee to heal, aren't you?"

Taken by surprise, Alexa stabbed herself with the needle she was using. She glared at Gray as she raised her finger to her mouth and sucked on the wounded digit. "Don't you know how to knock?" she demanded a minute later.

He grinned, satisfied that she was back to her old feisty ways. Good! This was how he liked her when she wasn't in his arms, moaning softly and driving him beyond reason and sanity.

"Your door was open. I didn't think you'd mind some company."

The look she gave him said otherwise.

Gray chuckled.

Alexa frowned at his peculiar behavior and returned her attention to the patch she was putting on a pair of Michael's jeans. She didn't want Gray in her room. She didn't want to be reminded of what had happened between them in the Jeep. And she most certainly didn't want to think about her uninhibited response to him, or the way he sent her common sense whirling into space at the mere thought of something similar happening again.

It *couldn't* happen again, she warned herself. He just wanted her body. He didn't want the woman or the emotions she would eagerly reveal if she lost total control. It was the same old story. She cared, and she gave. Only no one gave back. It hurt, more than she wanted to admit even to herself.

The feelings he inspired superseded anything she'd ever imagined between a man and a woman. It was like walking a tightrope whenever they were alone together. Even now, just a look from him sent her mind tumbling into a frantic search for a replay of the sizzling sensations.

"What do you know about interior decorating?" he asked, challenging her and knowing it.

"Enough." Her voice was flat as she thought of all the work she'd recently done in that arena for her father.

Oh, she'd enjoyed the unlimited budget and creative control. Only a crazy person or someone who truly hated decorating wouldn't enjoy that kind of freedom. What hadn't been a pleasure was her father's assumption that she owed him her time and talent. He hadn't asked, and he hadn't ever said thank you. Those two little words—thank you—would have meant the world to her once. Now, though, it would be a case of too little, too late. Appreciation had to be given like a gift, or it was valueless to the recipient.

"Good. Itemize your experience so I don't have to guess."

"Is that an order?" she asked tightly, not lifting her eyes from the sewing.

Gray cautioned himself to go easy on her. It was obvious she was still smarting from their afternoon together. "A request, pure and simple," he assured her.

She put the mending aside and looked at him as she spoke. "I coordinated the architectural plans, the primary contractor and the subcontractors for the house my father built last year on his estate in Santa Barbara. I then made the selections for the wall paint, the carpeting, draperies, shutters, lighting, fabrics for the furniture and accent pieces for five thousand square feet of living space. The decor was primarily desert southwest, which involves a lot of pastels and varying shades of white. There were several formal rooms to deal with, a master suite, four guest—"

"I get the picture," Gray interrupted, astonished by her monosyllabic delivery of an achievement that would have made anyone proud. Had he made a mistake with this decorating business? Curious about her attitude, he commented, "Sounds like you hated the job."

Blue-gray eyes went wide. "Why would you think that?"

He shrugged. "Let's start with your tone of voice."

"Forget my tone of voice," she advised, feeling awkward that he'd picked up on her distress. "The problem was personal. It had nothing to do with the actual job, which I enjoyed and did well. At least, that's what several friends said when they asked me to try my hand on their homes."

But not your father, he mentally filled in. Everything she said held a clue about the vulnerable state of her emotions. She didn't want to be taken advantage of, nor did she want to be treated like some empty-headed piece of fluff. Despite his insightfulness, Gray remained oblivious to her hunger for his love.

"Feel like taking another stab at it, but on a smaller scale?"

Alexa looked horrified. "Surely you don't want to redecorate your home?"

Surprised by both her question and her facial expression, Gray couldn't keep himself from asking, "Does that mean you like it?"

"I love it! It looks, feels like and *is* a real home. It's also elegant, comfortable, warm and welcoming. That's an unbeatable combination in my book. I wouldn't change a thing."

Gray added more information about her to the file tucked in the back of his mind. Home and family seemed almost sacred to her, but with her background, it was no wonder. Alexa was complicated, no doubt about it. He didn't understand everything that motivated her, but he *did* think he was finally starting to grasp what drove her so hard toward independence.

"Would you stop smirking at those books you're holding? You're starting to resemble a man with a fetish for fabric samples."

Gray grinned and dumped the stack on the end of her bed. "These belong to a decorator who flew in from San Francisco about a month ago. I'm trying to get some guest cottages I had built for visiting owners finished up. She'll be back Saturday, but I'm not ready for her. I flat don't have time for this stuff right now." He saw her interest and forged ahead. "As far as I'm concerned, decorating is a lot like art. I know what I like when I see it."

Alexa tugged a catalog from the stack and dragged it up to her lap. "I'm the same way. I tend to trust my instincts."

"The decorator will want final decisions on the cottages when she arrives. Is that enough time to figure out what we need?"

Alexa glanced up. Three days wasn't long enough, but she would manage. "You're cutting it close. Four cottages?"

"Four," he confirmed, mental fingers crossed.

"Carpeting and tile are already in, I hope."

"Last week."

"When can I see them?" she asked.

"First thing in the morning sound okay?"

"Perfect, but I need an idea of the colors you've used, as well as the style of furniture you've considered for each cottage."

Gray handed her a folder. "The carpet and tiles samples are in here, but the furniture style's your department."

Alexa flipped through the chosen samples before looking at Gray. "Do you want a dominant theme or something unique in each?"

"What's best? As I said, decorating's like art. I just know what I like when I see it."

She doubted his comment, although he seemed intent on having her believe it. Grayson Lennox was too discerning a man not to have extremely definite tastes about everything that affected his life and his environment. "What you *want* is what's best."

She smiled up at him, the first real smile he's seen in several hours. Relief rushed into his bloodstream like a powerful aphrodisiac.

"What are my choices?"

"You can extend the theme of the main house into each cottage, or you can have a theme that's consistent in each one even if it's different from the main house, or the variety of something unique in each one."

Gray thought about it for a moment. "I kind of like that desert southwest style you were talking about before."

"Good choice. The furniture is simple and straightforward designwise. And if your decorator has good suppliers, then we shouldn't have any trouble getting the wall hangings and other accent pieces."

Gray ambled over to the chair positioned beside the head of the bed. He sat down after relocating a stack of books from his library and a sewing kit to the nightstand. Wrapped up in her thoughts, she didn't really register Gray's close proximity at first.

"I appreciate this, Alexa. Money's no object, so just do whatever you think's right. I trust your judgment. With any kind of luck, maybe a few of the cottages will be ready in time for the annual picnic."

She sank back against the pillows, surprise in her eyes. "Minna mentioned the picnic, but I didn't think it was scheduled for anytime soon."

"About two and a half weeks from now, over the Fourth of July weekend. We ought to have more than two hundred people this year. Horse breeders fly in from all over the country. We book a block of rooms at a Stockton hotel, although most everybody spends the majority of the weekend out here at the ranch. Will has a team of drivers all set to handle the shuttle buses that take them back and forth between the ranch and the hotel."

Her expression serious, she promised, "I'll do the cottages, Gray, but I'll probably be gone before the picnic. My knee's getting better, so there'll be no reason for me to stay." She looked away. "Besides, I wouldn't want to be underfoot with that many people around."

He looked startled. "Underfoot? What the hell are you talking about?"

She tightened her grip on the sample book she held. "You don't need outsiders around when you're having your friends in for a party."

He leaned forward, resting his big hands on his knees. The movement put them nearly nose to nose. "We may not be lovers, but we're friends, aren't we?"

"After today, I don't know *what* we are," she answered, nervously smoothing the satin quilt beneath her fingertips.

He smiled at her honesty. That quality was one of the things he liked most about her. He doubted that she would ever lie or sugarcoat the truth.

"We're friends," he said firmly, "and ... almost lovers. Besides, I kind of hoped you'd want to be my hostess for the breeders' picnic."

"Oh, no. I couldn't." She loathed hostessing parties given for people she didn't know, despite her personal history.

"Why not?"

"I don't know these people, that's why not."

"You certainly didn't know all the people you've entertained for your father over the years."

"How'd you know about that?" *Minna,* she answered for herself.

"It doesn't matter how I know. I just do, that's all."

He smiled, his dark eyes glowing with satisfaction. She measured his expression, her resistance to the idea beginning to melt like chocolate under a hot sun.

"I don't know," she hedged.

"I'm not letting you off the hook, honey. I need your help, and I'm not too proud to ask for it."

They both recalled their conversation about Michael in the same instant. He'd said basically the same thing then.

"So? What's the verdict? Are you willing to pitch in around here for a few more weeks?"

Put that way, Alexa wondered how she could refuse. Being asked to help was certainly a vast improvement over announced expectations and drill-instructor orders. Besides, she wanted to stay, even if remaining played havoc with her heart and her sanity.

She sat up straighter against the headboard of the bed. "Tell me what I have to do to get ready for the picnic."

"Just keep the caterer and the party planner from Stockton on track. I had to referee one of their livelier disagreements last year. It wasn't a fun experience. I wound up wearing ten gallons of chocolate mousse for my trouble."

Gray scowled when he saw the delighted look on her face. Still, he went a step further, surprising them both with his next remark. "And one more thing, don't let our guests know what a jackass I can be some of the time. They think I'm a nice guy, and I don't want anybody leaving here thinking anything different."

She missed the underlying humor in his voice. "What in the world do you think I'd say to make them think anything of the sort?"

"You might tell them I jumped you in the Jeep this afternoon," he teased.

She paled, thinking that she would never admit to another soul how clumsily she'd handled what had happened between them. "You don't have to worry about that. Ever."

"Alexa?"

"Yes?"

"Look at me, honey."

She lifted her eyes, met his gaze and then nearly drowned in it. She stared at him, stunned by the strength and texture of her own feelings. She'd fallen in love with this man, a man who by his very nature was a loner.

"What is it?"

"Nothing," she whispered, still shaken by the enormity of the situation.

The smile left his face. "I didn't mean to try and push you into something you didn't want."

She flushed. "You didn't," she admitted, painfully honest despite the price her heart was paying as it thunked around in her chest. "I'm sorry if that's what I made you think. And I also apologize for losing my temper every time I turn around. I seem to be doing a lot of that lately."

"I'm sorry, too, more than you'll ever know. I keep telling myself not to rush you, but then I always manage to do something that makes you angry."

"I wasn't angry."

"Then what were you?" he asked softly.

"Afraid."

He looked shocked. "Of me?"

She shook her head.

He reached out and captured her hand, tugging her fingers from the sheet she was twisting and turning as though it had suddenly become a doorknob. "What're you afraid of, Alexa?"

Of always giving and never having anybody care enough to give back. Of wanting a man who doesn't want me. Of loving you so much that I'll never get over you.

Alexa sighed, and tears brimmed in her eyes. She blinked them away but not before Gray saw them. She felt his fingers tighten on her hand. The fierce pressure gave her the courage to continue. "You keep talking about trust when we...get close, but I don't know if I can trust anyone. I think that part of me is damaged or something."

"I don't know if I can fix it, but I'd like to try."

"Why?"

"I just need to make it right for you, honey. Maybe it's my way of saying thank you for what you've done with Michael." Liar! his conscience shrieked. Gray mentally flinched but kept speaking. "Whatever my motivation, just let me try, okay?"

Her spirits fell to an all-time low. Gratitude, but not love. Gratitude was better than being ignored, she tried to tell herself. Somehow, Alexa doubted it.

She tugged her hand free, her eyes empty of the sparkle that had been in them a few minutes earlier. All her self-protective instincts dutifully marched back to their sentry posts. Gray was too close again, and she wanted to throw herself into his arms too badly to tempt fate this late at night.

Gray took her withdrawal as his cue to leave, although he didn't really want to yet. He forced himself out of the chair. A few seconds later he paused in the doorway and turned to look at her.

He knew he would have her image firmly fixed in his mind all night. White satin tunic top and matching pants covered a body built for loving. Splashes of color tinted her high cheekbones. Her hair, loose and tousled, cascaded over her shoulders. She was an invitation to madness, and he wanted her so intensely that he would willingly risk that threat.

"I really *am* sorry."

"For what?" she asked tiredly.

"Everything."

"I'm sorry, too," she whispered, not really sure what they were both apologizing for this time, but needing desperately to prolong their time together.

"Forgiven, then?"

She nodded.

"I wasn't trying to hurt you today, and I wouldn't force you to do anything that doesn't feel right to you."

She smiled at him, all sad eyes, trembling mouth, soft satin and tumbled hair. "I know that, Gray. I knew it as soon as I calmed down and realized that neither one of us had considered the risks associated with being alone, especially in such an extraordinarily beautiful place. I didn't think."

"Sometimes thought is self-defeating," he bit out, every word like a bullet hitting a reinforced steel target.

She laughed, the sound a little too high-pitched to be genuine. "So is jumping out of an airplane without a parachute."

"Is that how you feel around me? Am I that much of a risk? Why do you feel the need for protection?"

"I might live through it that way," she said wryly. "I want you, Gray, even if you're wrong for me. Don't make me fight this battle alone. Help me a little, please."

She shifted uneasily on the bed when he didn't say anything. Her breasts moved invitingly against the satin she wore, the fabric abrading her nipples and bringing them tensely to life. She didn't notice the color that seeped into his face as he stared at her.

"God! You're a temptation."

Frantic, she searched her mind for a means of altering the mood of the room. She batted her eyelashes like a vamp, trying to lighten the intensity that always pulsed to life when they were alone together. "Resist your urges, big guy," she admonished in her best Mae West voice. "They'll be the end of us both if you don't."

He didn't respond to her attempt at levity. The hunger he felt for her had intensified too dramatically for him to let her think she could get away with it. "I wonder, Alexa. I really wonder if that's true. Maybe we should find out the truth one of these days."

He stepped out the room, obviously not expecting a reply. Alexa simply stared after him, aware that his game and his rules had left her, once again, at a distinct disadvantage.

Eight

Alexa spent the next four days immersed in plans for the cottages. She saw little of Gray, even though she used his library as her workroom.

When she *did* see him, she bit her tongue to keep from remarking on his noticeable absences during meal hours and in the evenings. Although neither one mentioned the incident in the Jeep again, neither were they able to ignore the palpable tension that continued to throb between them.

With the desert southwest theme as her decorating foundation, Alexa began preparing for the arrival of the interior decorator by sketching the floor plan of each cottage on poster board. She then selected the furniture, chose sturdy but attractive fabrics for each piece and decided on lighting fixtures and lamps.

She stapled fabric swatches and pictures of lamps and various other accent pieces down the sides of the poster board. By reserving a small section of each poster board for color coding, she experimented with colored pencils as she sought just the right blending of pastels and whites for each cottage.

She also made use of the numerous brochures and catalogs available to her, spending long hours deliberating over paintings, woven wall hangings and accent pieces for each cottage, despite the fact that her efforts would effectively reduce the decorator Gray had hired to an order taker. Pride and her desire to prove to him that she was up to the task spurred her on.

The decorator arrived early Saturday afternoon, her enthusiasm for her profession evident in both her flamboyant speech patterns and attire. An attractive woman in her late twenties, she didn't seem surprised by Alexa's role as decision maker on behalf of Grayson Lennox, nor did she seem offended that Alexa had already done her job for her.

The afternoon passed quickly, thanks to Alexa's preparation, attention to detail and the immediate rapport the two women developed. They chatted easily on a variety of subjects once they finished their work, discovering that they had mutual friends in Santa Barbara.

Gray made an appearance late in the afternoon. He asked a few polite questions about shipping dates, restated his desire that Alexa authorize the purchase of anything she considered appropriate for the cottages and then departed just as abruptly as he'd arrived.

Although she noticed the curiosity in the other woman's eyes, Alexa was grateful that she didn't question her relationship with Gray. She hated the idea of labeling herself as a casual friend, so she doggedly continued to focus on the cottages.

She escorted the smiling decorator to her rental car shortly before dusk, feeling both pleasure and a deep sense of satisfaction that all her ideas for the cottages had been well received and would be acted upon immediately. With a little

luck, they would be fully outfitted in time for the breeders'
picnic. A major coup, Alexa realized, as she tiredly returned to the house.

She spent most of Sunday lounging beside the pool situated behind the sprawling main house. Will and Minna
joined her, as did Michael and the two Wilcox boys. Gray
was conspicuously absent.

Alexa reminded herself that he didn't have to explain his
actions to anyone, but the fact that he hadn't bothered to
mention his destination or his reason for being away from
the ranch gnawed at her nerves. She silently berated herself
for falling in love with a man whose behavior made it very
clear that while he periodically needed her help, he definitely didn't want anything else from her.

The realization made her heart ache even more, but she
rallied her inner resources, forced her thoughts from Gray
and involved herself in those around her. Conversation
among the adults centered on the picnic, an annual event
Will and Minna had participated in since its inception five
years earlier and that celebrated the successful completion
of the horse-breeding season at the ranch.

Early Monday morning, following a particularly sleepless night, Alexa transferred her energies to the plans for the
picnic. The party consultant and caterer, a man and a
woman once happily married but who now conducted their
post-marital spats in front of their clients, arrived on time
but in separate cars.

Alexa took little comfort in the knowledge, shared con-
fidentially by Minna, that the two were extremely good at
their jobs. Otherwise, they would have been out of business long ago. She quietly cursed Gray for asking her to
hostess the picnic, then cursed herself for not heeding his
warning about the warring Lufkins. Anyone who made
Grayson Lennox nervous had to be hell on wheels. The party
consultant and caterer were that and more.

Acting as a combination referee, peacemaker and nego-
tiator, Alexa managed to hammer out a tentative menu, es-
tablish the party's theme, the selection of both daytime and
evening entertainment, and settle on the size of the staff that
would be hired to serve food and other refreshments, as well
as clean up after the guests.

Exhausted after a day-long battle of wills and explosive
temperaments, Alexa indulged in a quiet dinner in the
kitchen before excusing herself for the night. She show-
ered, changed into a long pale pink nightgown, and crawled
into bed just after sundown, but an active subconscious refused to let her sleep more than a few hours.

Still, she lingered in bed, listening for any telltale sounds
of activity in the house. All she heard was the steady tick-
ing of her travel alarm clock, which revealed that it was near
midnight when she glanced at it. Her thoughts wandered to
Gray and she absently wondered if he had come home yet.
Suddenly frustrated with her ungovernable thoughts, she
told herself that his activities, whatever they were, didn't
concern her.

Restless, she soon slipped from her bed and carefully
made her way out to the balcony. She left her cane propped
against the wall near her bed. Wrapping her arms around
herself, she leaned against the balcony railing, her eyes
closed as she inhaled the fragrant night air.

Gray stood in the shadows of the balcony. The air froze
in his lungs the instant he saw Alexa step out of the open
double doors of her room. Moonlight spilled across the
railing and onto the balcony, spotlighting her as she stood a
scant six feet away.

He didn't miss the tumbled disarray of her tangled hair
spilling down her back, or the subtle shifting of her full
breasts beneath her nightgown each time she took a breath.
Nor could he ignore the revealing silhouette of her body,
which was barely shielded by the simply designed, low-cut

silk gown that was suspended from her shoulders by two narrow strips of fabric.

Gray moved forward, only vaguely aware of his actions and clad in nothing but jeans. He reached her just as she released a heavy sigh. The sound was lonely, almost sad, a melancholy echo of emotions he knew and understood all too well.

Alexa leaned forward, still unaware that she wasn't alone. Resting her hands on the railing that circled the upper level of the house, she turned her head from side to side, trying to ease the tenseness in her neck and shoulders.

Gray sensed her vulnerability, and he felt her tension. He grudgingly acknowledged a corresponding vulnerability and tension within himself. Lifting his hands to her shoulders, he felt the brief stiffening of her body and heard the swift intake of her breath at his touch. He then heard her softly murmured groan of appreciation as he slowly and ever so tenderly began to massage her shoulders.

"You're awfully tense," he noted after several quiet moments marked only by the sound of their breathing and the crickets harmonizing on the lawn below.

"Mm."

"Long day?"

"*Five* long days," she corrected, her voice subdued. "I should hate you, you know."

He paused, briefly considered her remark, then chuckled. He deserved her soft-voiced rancor. "The Lufkins."

"Exactly."

"Unbelievable, aren't they?"

"I can't imagine how they managed to stay married for more than a month."

"They didn't."

She turned slightly and glanced at him. "You're kidding."

"Nope. They split after six days, or so the story goes." He resumed the massage once she turned to look out across the pool and lawn.

"Why do they continue working together?"

"Who knows why people who love each other do anything? I doubt *they* know. Otherwise, they'd have called it quits years ago."

"Years? You mean they've been divorced for a long time?"

"Fifteen years, I think."

"Good heavens!"

He laughed, the sound rich. Alexa felt chill bumps rise on her flesh at the intimacy of both the sound and the moment. She shivered slightly.

"Cold?" Gray asked, his hands curving protectively over her shoulders.

She shook her head, enjoying the warm breeze that caressed her face and the feel of Gray's hands as he began to move them up and down her arms again. She didn't want him to stop touching her quite yet, although she suspected that she was simply torturing herself with what could never be.

He kept stroking, his big hands firm but gentle as he kneaded the knots from her shoulders, neck and upper back. Alexa let her head fall forward and exhaled softly, captured by the sensual spell Gray had already begun to weave around her. She savored not just his touch but also the serenity of the moment.

"Feel good?" he asked, striving for a nonthreatening tone to compensate for the almost violent hunger now storming his mind and body.

She smiled, a new and very seductive kind of tension filtering through her. "Feels like heaven."

He lowered his head until he could inhale the faint jasmine scent of her skin and hair. His hands stilled. Tugging her backward so that she rested against his chest, he brought his arms around her, his hands coming to rest against her abdomen. The undersides of her silk-covered breasts brushed his muscular forearms each time she took a breath. The torturous feeling seared his soul and made his hands tremble.

"Heaven," he repeated, his voice raw. "Just like you."

She struggled for control, despite the erratic cadence of her heart and the tingling sensations targeting the pulse points in her body. She felt Gray's strength in the solid muscles of his bare chest. Leaning against him, she consciously fought the tantalizing sensations of his dense chest hair against her back which enticed her senses and subverted nearly all her common sense and good intentions.

Trembling, she finally managed to whisper, "You've been away a lot the last few days."

"A ranch doesn't run itself," he answered reflexively. Gray paused, his heart tripping unsteadily against his chest, then made himself admit, "Hell! Being gone had nothing to do with the ranch. It was the only way I could keep my hands off you."

She slowly turned in his arms and looked up at him in the dim light. Desire thrummed like a current of electricity between them. Alexa felt curiously bemused and quite lightheaded, but not at all shocked by his remark. "I'm driving you out of your own home."

He threw back his head, closed his eyes, inhaled deeply, then released the air caught in his lungs in short bursts. "You, honey, are slowly driving me out of my mind. Let's get that straight once and for all."

"I should leave." She felt his hands tighten on her waist the instant the words left her mouth.

"That's not what I want, and you know it," he said harshly.

"But, Gray, if..." The words trailed off toward oblivion, the same destination her mind seemed intent on seeking.

He drew her closer, bringing them into intimate hip-to-hip contact with one hand, while he carefully pressed her silk-covered breasts to his chest with the other. He groaned at the promise implicit in the contact, the sound escaping his gritted teeth before he could stop it.

Alexa inhaled sharply, thoroughly rattled by the feel of Gray's arousal and the streamers of fire invading every groove and hollow of her body. She felt her knees start to buckle; the muscles in her legs suddenly turned soft and malleable. Breathlessly, she admitted, "It's not what I want either, but maybe it's what's best."

He pulled her even more firmly into his arms, his embrace powerful, possessive, even fierce. The feel of her flush against him fired already combustible need and sent a shudder rippling through his body. "Who's to say what's best?" he demanded, not angry, just painfully frustrated. "I just know that I want you. I've wanted you since the very first."

She reached up, her fingertips hesitant as she caressed his hard cheeks, strong chin, and then lingered to trace the contours of his sensual mouth. He was everything she'd ever dreamed of in a man. She wanted him. Each instinct, each sense she possessed cried out to him for fulfillment.

And, oddly, she no longer feared being overwhelmed by him. In fact, she welcomed the very idea, because she sensed that he would only overwhelm her with passion. She felt certain that she would still retain her personhood, her right to be whole and valuable as an individual. She lowered her fingertips to the pulse point at his throat, the wildly pounding force that tremored against his skin and branded her just as intensely as the ridge of hard flesh pressed so intimately to her lower abdomen.

Gray's eyes fell closed, the thick lashes shaped like feathery dark half-moons evident even in the near darkness of the night. He stopped breathing for an endless moment. This was what he'd dreamed of, carved with a hunger so devastating that it stunned him. Her touch, her gentleness, he wanted everything she had to give.

He opened his eyes and looked down at her, a wealth of anguished need in his dark gaze. "Give me your mouth, Alexa. I'm starving for the taste of you."

She melted under the heat of his words. Fire danced along her skin, flirting with her sanity and threatening her ability to respond on any level but a physical one. Any residual resistance she might have felt as a result of their time together instantly drained out of her.

"You still say the most outrageous things," she whispered, more to herself than to him.

Tired of fighting, tired of being on guard all the time, tired of being alone, Alexa lifted her head and felt his mouth close possessively over her lips. She shook under the most encompassing, most shattering contact she had ever before experienced. She held tightly to him, welcoming the thrusting intrusion of his tongue as it swept past her teeth and bathed the interior of her mouth with his taste.

Gray savored every aspect of her responsiveness. He drank greedily from her eager mouth, moaned deep in his throat at the feel of the stiffened crests of her nipples stabbing at his chest and grew harder still when he felt the answering sway of her hips as she accepted the suggestive pressure of his.

He found the narrow straps of her gown with shaking fingers and eased them from her shoulders. When Alexa didn't protest, he lifted his lips from her sweet mouth and separated their bodies for the few moments that it took to peel the pale silk gown from her breasts.

"Perfect," he breathed as he stared down at her, his fingers dark against her breasts as he stroked her golden skin. "Absolutely perfect."

Her eyes drifted closed and she smiled, her expression languid. Her insides flowed like molten gold, and she responded instinctively to him. Alexa lifted her arms, looped them around his neck and molded herself to the hard lines of his virile body.

She sighed shakily just before he took her mouth and shaped his hands over her narrow back. Nearly overcome by the force of the emotion swirling through her, she met demand with demand and he inched his hands slowly forward again toward her breasts. He aroused her nipples to such hard beads of pleasure that she moaned aloud, startling herself with the sound and her utter lack of restraint.

Time ceased to matter, except as a measurement of the heady, almost urgent pleasure that had become a part of their thundering heartbeats and feverish bodies. Gray took pleasure in the frantic sweep of Alexa's fingertips across his shoulders and down his back, just as he relished the freedom her gown, now caught at her hips, provided as he gave in to his instincts and caressed every inch of her exposed skin.

He didn't allow their lips to part as he leaned down and gathered Alexa into his arms. Walking into the guest room, his footsteps sure as he approached the bed, he paused near the nightstand and lowered her to her feet. Only then did he break their connection, but only for a brief moment.

He steadied her when she lost her balance, drawing her into his arms and holding her for a lingering moment. Her long hair tangled in his fingers as he held her, and he couldn't resist the temptation of gathering the fragrant mass into his hands and pressing it to his face. He inhaled deeply, filling his senses with the scent of her.

Alexa rested her forehead against his shoulder, breathless and shaking with anticipation. Before she could muster even a simple thought, they were sprawled across the bed, limbs tangled, mouths avid, and senses shattering.

Gray was near the edge. Soon, he wouldn't be able to stop himself. He rolled onto his back and pulled Alexa atop him, his manner unexpectedly playful as he nipped at her lips and then soothed the tender area with the tip of his tongue. He forced himself to slow down, forced himself to give Alexa a final opportunity to make the choice for herself.

"I want you."

"I want you," she responded in kind, heart pounding and face flushed with passion.

Her response detonated a charge of pleasure inside him. "I don't want to hurt you." He reached up, cupping her face with tender hands. "Don't let me hurt you, Alexa."

She cocked her head to one side, reminding him of the wary little fox he'd first met in what seemed like a lifetime ago. Once again, she seemed to sense some undefined danger. He also knew that she was tempted by it.

"You, more than anyone, have the power to hurt me," she admitted, honest as always.

Gray felt his heart pause in midbeat, but he didn't say anything. He watched her, his dark gaze narrowed as she slowly slid free of his embrace and moved off him.

Aware that there was more to his comment than she first realized, Alexa studied him, a mixture of tenderness and sadness in her expression. This was his way, she suddenly realized, of telling her that he couldn't ever love her. That gift had already been given to another woman, and she'd taken it with her to her grave.

Alexa trembled, but she forced herself to remain in control. From a distant corner of her mind came the certain knowledge that she couldn't give herself to a man who still loved another woman.

Very carefully, as though to spare herself just a little of the pain that was already starting to smother her, and very gently, she said, "I won't be a substitute for Jenny. I couldn't stand it if I thought you were using me that way."

Shock, followed swiftly by anger, defused his arousal as effectively as a cold shower. He swore, harshly and explicitly. Alexa flinched, but she didn't try to stop him as he jerked himself up off the bed.

He towered over her, long muscled legs spread wide, broad chest bare, almost threatening. He glared while she sat up and tugged her nightgown back into place. Her breasts ached. Her limbs felt weighted down by the lethargy of slowly fading desire. When her nipples beaded against the silk of her gown, she saw the color leave Gray's face.

He remained silent for several moments. All the while, his conscience hammered at him. He *had* used her, but not in the way she thought.

He needed her for Michael, not just for himself. He needed all the beautiful parts of her that she shared so readily with those who touched her heart. He even needed her fiery temper and her willingness to stand up to him when he was wrong. He needed her strength and her softness, even if his fear of loving her tortured him on an hourly basis. But if he let himself love her, he reasoned emotionally, then he risked losing her. His heart nearly stopped at the thought of that happening. Gray knew he wouldn't survive the loss of another loved one.

"Jenny is part of the past," he said in a low, intense voice. "I loved her when she was alive, but life goes on. I'll never forget her, Alexa, but she isn't here in this room, nor is she in my thoughts when I have you in my arms. And if I've used you, then it was only to help Michael."

"I want to believe you."

"You can," he assured her, taking a step toward the bed.

She raised one slim hand to halt his advance. He stopped, caution and uncertainty in his dark eyes. Alexa saw his vulnerability and longed to reach out to him, but she couldn't pay the high price attached to the act.

"Please be sure, Gray. Give yourself a little more time. Be absolutely certain that you know the difference between the past and the present, between Jenny Lennox and Alexa Rivers. I couldn't bear it if you were wrong."

Gray exhaled heavily, nodded, then turned and walked out of the room. He took Alexa's love with him, but he was too blinded by his own confused emotions to recognize that fact.

Gray found Alexa in the dining room the next morning, idly flipping through the pages of Stockton's daily newspaper and sipping the last of her morning tea. He strode into the room, moving with the confidence that only a man secure with his own masculinity can achieve. He tossed his dusty Stetson onto an empty chair, helped himself to a mug of coffee from the urn Minna always left on the sideboard and dropped into the chair at the head of the table.

Alexa folded the newspaper and faced him, her chin raised just enough to tell him that she wasn't cowed by his presence and that she meant everything she'd said the night before. Her nervousness only showed briefly in the rattle of her teacup as she placed it in the saucer in front of her.

"I've got to go to Dallas."

She arched a slender brow, surprised that he was even announcing his plans. She wondered how they concerned her.

"It's an overnight trip. Feel like packing a bag and coming along for the ride? You might enjoy yourself."

Trust him to always do the unexpected, she thought. She searched the enigmatic expression on his face long and hard, but she couldn't find a clue about his true feelings to her potential reaction to his invitation.

"Dallas?" she murmured, as though he'd asked her to take a trip to the dark side of the moon.

"Dallas," he confirmed. "Home of the Centurian Club Annual Charity Auction and Ball."

Interest seeped into her expression. She knew about the Centurian Club, although she'd never attended any of its functions. Her father traveled in the same moneyed circles as many of the club members, wealthy entrepreneurs who could afford to give generously to their favorite charities and who also owned some of the finest horse-racing stock in the world.

"Well, honey, what's the verdict?" He sounded flip. He felt anything but. "Do you trust me enough for an overnight excursion, or do I need to assure you that we'll have separate bedrooms?"

"I trust you, but I'd still want my own bedroom."

Annoyance flickered briefly in his eyes. "That's a start, I suppose."

She ignored his sarcasm. "When would we leave?" she asked, as though her calendar was jammed with previous engagements. If he could be cool, then so could she.

"First thing tomorrow morning. Care to tag along?" He silently cursed himself for asking a second time. Now he sounded eager and his pride was already singed enough where Alexa Rivers was concerned.

She smiled, a brilliant show of even white teeth and sparkling eyes. Gray almost dropped his coffee mug at the sight of the dazzling display.

"I'm a little too old for *tagging*. But if you're inviting me to accompany you to a party as your date, then...I accept," she said, wanting to make him squirm a little.

Gray downed the last of his coffee, shoved his empty mug onto the table and got to his feet. "Honey, that's exactly what I'm asking. We'll leave just after dawn, so be ready."

"Yes, sir! Anything else, sir?"

He closed in on her like a man riding herd on an unpredictable filly. He leaned down, planted a hand on each side of her body and smiled seductively. "Oh, yes, there's something else, but it'll only happen when you're ready." With that announcement, he raised a hand, lifted her chin with one long finger and planted a noisy kiss on her shock-parted lips. "I'd linger, but the temptation to take you right down on the dining-room floor is too much for this mere mortal to resist."

He straightened, smiling when Alexa simply sputtered incoherently. "The party's formal, so pack something sexy." He winked at her. "Something that'll make my bones ache. On second thought, maybe you shouldn't. I've been in this condition for so long now, I'll probably end up in traction before the month's up."

Alexa stopped sputtering and grinned, the expression on her face just shy of mischievous. "I've always wanted to go to one of the Centurian Club's black-tie affairs."

With a muttered oath, Gray stalked out of the dining room. Alexa could tell by the rigidity of his wide shoulders that she'd managed to set his teeth on edge with her last remark. His ego was already big enough, she reminded herself. Grayson Lennox needed to learn a little humility. It would do him good to think he was a minor attraction compared to the charity auction and ball.

The following evening, Alexa stood in front of the mirror in her bedroom of the suite Gray had booked at the Dallas Concorde. As she put the last-minute touches on her makeup and fastened a chunky gold choker around her neck that matched the earrings and bracelet she wore, she gave herself a quick once-over. Satisfied that the strapless black taffeta dress would be appropriate for the evening, she smoothed down the ruffled tiers of fabric that formed the short skirt and thought about the last twelve hours.

Rendered speechless when Gray, dressed in white linen slacks, leather deck shoes and a beautifully woven gray pullover, had pulled up in front of the house that morning in a sleek red Ferrari, she didn't find her tongue until they'd boarded a chartered Lear jet that immediately whisked them off to Dallas.

"You're just full of surprises, aren't you?" she commented, still a bit disconcerted as they sipped freshly brewed coffee while a steward served them a hot breakfast.

Gray's smile was as mischievous as hers had been the day before. "At least I know you aren't after me for my money."

"After your money?" she exclaimed. "Of all the egotistical, conceited—"

"I know," he said equably, the smile still dancing in his eyes and quelling her momentary irritation with him.

A limo collected them at the airport terminal. The drive into Dallas took less than thirty minutes, sufficient time for Alexa to fully grasp the meaning of the word *big*. They lunched in the five-star restaurant perched high atop the Concorde before Gray excused himself after escorting Alexa to their suite, explaining that he had business to conduct prior to the evening festivities.

Alexa napped, did her nails, fretted whether or not she had selected the right dress for the party, bathed and dried and arranged her hair. She then worried a little more that she might be tempting fate—and Gray—in the daring black taffeta creation designed by a couturier she'd long admired.

Dismissing her thoughts, she tugged the bodice of her dress up another inch or so, hastily tucked tissues, lipstick and a compact into her beaded evening bag and walked to the bedroom door. Although she didn't really need it very often now, she collected her cane just before she stepped into the sitting room.

Gray stood in front of the wall of windows on the opposite side of the room, his attention on the panoramic view of the skyscraper-filled city. Dressed in classic black evening clothes, he took her breath away as he slowly turned and gave her one of his thousand-watt smiles.

She hesitated, uncertainty suddenly swamping her. She knew the blunt, rough-edged rancher from central California, the man who wore body-hugging faded denims, scarred leather boots and chambray work shirts. The same man who could be fierce when crossed and infinitely tender when the situation called for it. This man, who looked as though he'd just stepped from the pages of a high-fashion men's magazine, was as unfamiliar to her as a stranger on a downtown street corner. Good manners somehow emerged from the slushy confines of her mind and saved the day.

"You look very handsome."

Gray took a step forward, his broad smile faltering. "And you look so damned incredible that I'll probably dismember any guy who gets within a hundred feet of you."

She laughed nervously. "Thank you, I think."

"I should be thanking *you*, Alexa," he said, his smile disappearing as he approached her. He towered over her despite the heels she wore. "Thanking you for trusting me enough to make this trip with me."

She didn't move, hardly even dared to breathe, as he lifted his hands, reached out and lightly ran his fingertips across her bare shoulders and down her arms.

"You are truly exquisite."

"I don't know about that," she whispered, flushing as a result of the naked hunger reflected in his eyes. She took a deep breath, realized just how she hoped the night would end and exhaled shakily as an explicitly intimate image popped into her mind. She shook her head, the confused gesture meant to clear her blistering thoughts. The image faded but didn't disappear altogether as she looked up at Gray.

"I'll have to do more than dismember if you walk out of here with that look in your eyes, honey."

His husky tone jarred her back to reality. "Wrong! There's absolutely no need to play the bully, Gray. I know who my date is tonight, and he has my undivided attention."

Gray moved even closer, his physical presence and the force of his personality staggering her senses. He lowered his gaze to the cleavage revealed by her dress and shuddered visibly. "I want more than one night."

She registered the frantic pace of her own pulse and felt heat surge into her bloodstream. "We'll be late if we don't leave now."

He gracefully accepted her verbal sidestep, although the languid smile easing across his striking face told her that the issue was far from settled. He took her arm, led her from the suite and out for a night of revelation and magic.

The auction, held under an enormous circus tent designed to house five hundred guests at a ranch on the outskirts of Dallas, was an elegant, laughter-filled event. The festivities began just as Alexa and Gray arrived. People greeted Gray with an easygoing attitude reserved for a respected friend and welcomed Alexa with typical Texas hospitality.

As he watched her, Gray decided that Alexa would never meet a stranger. He admired her relaxed manner, her ability to fit in anywhere, but most of all he admired the lack of pretense in her personality. She was a natural, totally at home on a working horse farm like Lennox Ranch or at a five-thousand-dollar-a-plate dinner for charity. Glancing around their table, he realized that no one was immune to her innate charm.

While Alexa enjoyed the upbeat energy and enthusiasm of the evening, she couldn't keep her eyes off Gray. She watched and listened, impressed with his articulate knowledge of the horse-breeding world and his sophisticated demeanor. After a moment of thought, she realized that she shouldn't be the least bit surprised by this aspect of his multifaceted personality. Grayson Lennox, like many of the powerful men she'd met over the years, was confident, secure and a personal success. He had every right to command the respect and admiration of his peers.

She abandoned her mental musings when the tone of the party abruptly changed. Excitement heightened the pitch of the voices around her. Strobe lights flashed across the tent's vaulted ceiling and then down to the black stallion being led onto a specially constructed ramp next to the auctioneer's podium.

Gray stood, leaned down briefly and dropped a kiss on Alexa's forehead. "Don't go away. I'll be right back."

She watched him confidently thread his way through the crowd and take a position in the area reserved for bidders. The woman seated beside her murmured something like, "You two make the most striking couple. I hope ya'll will invite us to the wedding." Startled, Alexa tried to set the record straight, but enthusiastic applause drowned her out.

The horse was called Destiny and the bidding was like a well-orchestrated battle among generals. Gray ended the fray with his final bid, an astounding sum of money to anyone who didn't comprehend Destiny's potential as a sire. The recipient of the crowd's enthusiastic applause, Gray paused briefly at the auctioneer's microphone, a practice established earlier by those who wished to donate to the charity of their choice.

"On behalf of Alexa Rivers, I'm pledging fifteen percent of Destiny's purchase price to Rivers House, a home for children in Santa Barbara, California. Ms. Rivers is my guest this evening, and she manages the trust set up to fund Rivers House.''

Gray made his way back to the table as the applause died down. He saw tears sparkling on the tips of Alexa's eyelashes and felt the staggering pleasure of a man who has made the most important person in his world happy. He didn't give her a chance to say anything. Instead, he drew her from her chair, escorted her to the dance floor at the far side of the tent and tugged her into his arms for the first dance of the evening.

They moved together like lovers preparing for consummation, the throbbing beat of the music an integral part of their seductive foreplay. Their bodies intimately aligned and their hearts beating as one, they were oblivious to the other couples who joined them on the dance floor, the tiny lights sparkling like a canopy of stars overhead and the knowing smiles of old friends and new acquaintances.

"You should have warned me," Alexa finally murmured. "I nearly fell off my chair when you announced your donation."

"I did it because I respect your commitment to the children." He tightened his arms around her, his body growing increasingly aroused as they danced.

Alexa felt his heat and his need. Instead of drawing away, she shifted against him. She wanted him to know that she welcomed his passion. She wanted whatever he could give her, wanted him because she loved him and couldn't bear the thought of walking away from him without experiencing what she was certain would be a kaleidoscope of feelings and emotions beyond her wildest dreams.

She knew she would leave the ranch soon, but not until after the breeders' picnic. She would hold the inevitable at bay just a little longer. She had decided she owed herself the knowledge of what it would be like to make love with the man who had captured her heart. And she owed him the honesty of her desire for him.

She lifted her head from Gray's shoulder when his footsteps slowed. Standing in the center of the crowded dance floor, she could see the fire blazing in his eyes, could feel the subtle tremors shuddering through his body. An answering ripple of pure desire lanced through her slender frame. His eyes flared wide, a wash of color suffused his hard cheeks, and his fingers, which had fallen to her waist, tightened perceptibly.

A gong sounded, startling them both. The crowd quieted briefly as a long line of waiters and waitresses streamed into the tent bearing dome-covered platters. They both heard the laughter, champagne corks popping and voices raised in a variety of toasts, but only as a peripheral sound at the edge of the sensory and physical space they occupied.

Gray slipped his arm around Alexa and guided her toward their table. He glanced down at her when she hesitated halfway there. They stared at one another, an unspoken conversation raging between them.

Gray finally urged, "Say the words, Alexa."

"I'd like to go back to the hotel," she whispered.

He nodded. The intensity of her blue-gray eyes tore at him, shredded the tattered remnants of his control. He wanted the desire shimmering in her eyes translated to a tangible declaration of intent, but her reluctance to say anything more prompted him to tighten his grip on her waist as he led her back to their table for her purse and cane.

Nine

——

They stood a few feet apart in the sitting room of the suite, blue-gray and deep brown eyes smoldering as they silently watched one another.

So tense that his muscles literally ached, Gray hastily shed his jacket, jerked off his tie and released the top button and two studs of his dress shirt with shaking fingers. He dropped everything onto a nearby chair, his gaze still riveted on Alexa.

Trembling, she used the back of the same chair to brace herself as she leaned down to unstrap her heeled sandals. She stepped out of them and straightened, unaware that her breasts were in danger of spilling from the bodice of her dress.

An odd sound burst from Gray and she froze. She cast a cautious glance at his face. His eyes were dark, a muscle kept jumping in his jaw, and his hands were clenched and white-knuckled at his sides. A storm tide seemed to rise in his expression.

"What's wrong?"

Desire relentlessly drove at him, but he made himself speak. "You're coming out of your clothes, and I'm having a hell of a time keeping my hands to myself."

She took a sharp breath, shocked by his anger before she realized it wasn't anger at all. It was the culmination of weeks of holding back, of reining in need and something she wasn't even sure how to define. Moving toward him, she took the few steps that placed them within a scant six inches of one another. Raising her hands, she finished the job he'd begun, her deft fingers releasing the remaining studs of his shirt. She hesitated at his cummerbund, then glanced at him.

Gray's features, drawn taut across his face, reflected the agony of unstable control. "Alexa, say something. I'm not made of stone, and you're making it almost impossible for me to keep my hands off you."

She looked up, the expression on her face both reflective and understanding. "I don't want you to keep your hands off me. I want to feel them on me. And I know you aren't made of stone," she finished with a kind of calm certainty that would have normally shocked her. But she wasn't shocked, not any longer and definitely not at herself. She knew that whatever happened between them would be right.

He suddenly dragged her against his chest, bringing his mouth down so quickly that she didn't have time to think, let alone draw a breath of air. She could only feel, and what she felt surged into her bloodstream, dark, mysterious and thoroughly intoxicating.

Gray parted her lips with the bold thrust of his tongue. He hurled himself directly into her heat, basking in it until he thought his heart would stagger to a stop. He felt tremors shake her and forced himself to slow down. At the rate he was going, he would take her where they stood, with no preliminaries, no thought to the promises he'd made to himself about their first time together.

He reluctantly dragged his mouth from her lips. Bending down, he picked her up and carried her into the bedroom. She curled against his body, a soft sigh washing across the side of his face as he held her. He tightened his embrace, feeling possessive, greedy.

She was his now. His for as long as he could convince her to remain at Lennox Ranch. After that... He ruthlessly banished the thought from his mind. He didn't want to think about anything after Alexa. Stopping beside the bed, he carefully lowered her to her feet, instinctively careful of her nearly healed right knee.

Alexa sensed an almost unnatural caution in Gray. It struck her as completely out of character. She didn't want caution; she wanted Grayson Lennox, the forceful, temperamental, single-minded and passionate man she'd come to know and love.

She reached up and slid her fingertips across his cheeks. "I'm here because I want to be with you, Gray. Don't be careful with me and don't hold back. We've both waited long enough. All I want is to make love with you."

He shook his head and smiled. "You say the damnedest things, honey."

She smiled back at him, thinking vaguely that that was her line, and tugged his head down to her mouth. She felt his hands on the zipper of her dress. Tempting him with the almost innocent experimentation of a young woman testing newly discovered seductive powers, she touched her tongue to his lips, sweeping the tip back and forth across his mouth until a groan escaped him.

Gray tugged her dress down, easing it over her hips and discovering in the process that all she wore was a short black slip and dark panty hose. Repressed air burned in his lungs. His body leaped in response to the knowledge of how little actually separated them. His hands shook as he held her. He said a quick prayer for control.

Alexa moaned, a small sound in the back of her throat that incited a new burst of fire in Gray when he sucked her curious tongue into his mouth and ran his fingertips down the silken smoothness of her naked spine. She drew in a sharp breath, arched against him and felt the hard ridge of flesh still trapped beneath his clothing. She eased her hands between their straining bodies and found his zipper. When her fingers became clumsy, she let out a moan of pure frustration, a sound Gray tasted as well as felt.

Her faint jasmine scent engulfed him, sent his senses spinning into space. He helped her, unable to muster the control he'd promised himself he would use with her. He hurriedly stripped off his own clothing, discarding it on the floor beside Alexa's dress. Clad now in black briefs that did little to conceal his desire, he helped her peel away the remaining barriers that covered her and then tumbled her onto her back across the center of the bed.

Their mouths locked together, arms circled, hands clutched almost frantically because they couldn't get enough of one another. Alexa met his demand with her own. Running her hands freely across his heated body, she left hot little pinpoints of flame in her wake.

Gray responded in kind, lavishing her with the attention Alexa had until now believed would never be hers. Her heart sang, her nerves arced like electrified wires that had suddenly gone wild, and her ability to reason was swept away on a tide of sensuality so intense she thought she would die if it ever ended.

They sipped and nipped at one another, their lips and tongues engaged in a sensual exercise that had no rules but the satisfaction inherent in the utter rapaciousness of the act. Gray stroked the undersides of her breasts with his long, blunt fingers as his mouth lingered over hers, then traced a line down her stomach to the tangle of golden silk at her thighs. He dipped his questing fingers even lower, finding tantalizing receptivity. His heart stopped beating for a long moment, then resumed its primitive cadence, deafening him with the echo beating at his senses.

Alexa arched almost violently at the intimate exploration, as sensation after sensation ripped through her body and shredded her nerves. Gray gathered her close, burying his face in the fragrant curve of her neck as he stroked her higher and higher and struggled to tamp down the flames encompassing him. Feverish with need, he eased down beside her, bathing her breasts with the rasping wet strokes of his tongue as his fingers continued to taunt her tender flesh.

Alexa's fingertips drifted down Gray's chest, periodically tangling in the dense hair that mapped his upper body and abdomen. She traced the hard muscles of his stomach, felt them clench and unclench as she grew increasingly more bold. She realized that there were no rules when love bound you to another.

Freed by that insight, she grasped him, felt his body jerk in reply to her gently rhythmic stroking, heard his unsteady breathing. He eventually raised his lips from the bounty of her breasts, his breathing even more ragged now, the expression on his face implying profound pain. He watched her closely, mesmerized by the honesty of her delight in the rapt expression on her face as they both touched, enticed and very nearly drove each other into the arms of madness.

There was an utter rightness about this intimacy between them, and it touched the core of his heart. He shuddered under the impact of it. At the edge of any control he might have once had, Gray reluctantly moved free of her fingers.

He absorbed Alexa's soft murmur of protest with his mouth as he reached out and retrieved the protection she deserved in the drawer of the nightstand beside his bed. After a brief moment, he moved over her. Using his arms for support, he eased down between her thighs, his sex heavy and full and throbbing with the need for release inside her.

"Thank you," she whispered, touched by the thoughtfulness of his behavior.

He framed her face with his hands, his voice hushed as he said, "I meant it when I told you I didn't want to ever hurt you."

She nodded and brought their mouths together with a gentle tug on his shoulders. He thrust into the melting moistness of her body, groaning when he felt the sensual pull of tiny muscles and incredible heat. She cried out and her fingernails scored his back.

Gray recognized her cry for what it was...an expression of joy, an expression akin to relief that the waiting was finally over, an expression that matched the sentiments filling his mind before he abandoned all control.

Ecstasy shimmered just beneath her skin, then rose like the consuming waves of a relentless tide. She shivered under the power, the urgency and the headiness sweeping over her. No one would ever be more important to her than Gray. She was certain of it, more certain than she'd ever been of anything in her entire life.

He set their pace, sweeping her along with him until he launched them both into oblivion. The madness that had threatened her sanity and her soul now encompassed her. He didn't release her mouth until he bent to suckle and savor her nipples.

He tantalized and teased as he swept back and forth from one breast to the other, his teeth rough and arousing against the pink crests. They vaulted together into the stars and exploded like a planet destined to disintegrate in a shower of fire across the heavens.

Emotion scorched her soul, devastated her grasp on reality. Alexa clung to Gray, the aftershocks tremoring through her body matching the ones rippling through his. She loved him. She would love him until she drew her last breath, but she was reluctant to say the words aloud. Instinct assured her that Gray wouldn't welcome the declaration.

He remained embedded within her even as he rolled them to one side. He watched her as he held her, saw the slight glazing of her eyes as she looked at him.

"I didn't know, Gray. I really didn't know."

"Didn't know what?"

"That making love could make you feel so free."

He laughed, his chest rumbling with the sound. "That was just the beginning, honey."

"Will I survive it?" she wondered aloud, her eyes filled with emotion.

"Why do I suddenly get the impression that you're not..." His voice trailed off, an indication of his growing concern. It had never really occurred to him whether or not Alexa was experienced. Somehow, it hadn't mattered, until now.

She knew what he wanted to know. Lifting her shoulders in a delicate shrug, she turned her face into the curve of his neck. "This was only my second time."

He tensed. "Ever?"

"Ever," she confirmed. She raised her head and smiled. "I loved making love with you, Gray." *And I love you so much that I ache with the feeling.*

Gray saw the look on her face. It was too transparent to ignore. He felt a pang of genuine regret when he realized what she needed to hear from him. He loved her. The reality of his feelings struck him like a thunderbolt and he shuddered with the impact. How could he risk it? He remained silent, although the flicker of disappointment in her eyes pierced his heart.

"You should've told me."

"Why?"

"Because I would've taken more time, been more careful."

"You weren't careful?"

"Of course, but..."

She shifted, forced him onto his back and positioned herself atop him. Making love had given her a sense of freedom that dissolved any inhibitions she might have once felt around him. "Show me how careful you should've been, Gray," she urged as she nipped at his chin.

Not quite over the stunning impact of her admission, he clamped his hands over her wriggling hips to hold her still. He wanted to make love with her until he died in her arms, but he needed to know more, although he denied the significance of his curiosity when his conscience kicked at him. "Was the first time that bad?"

"Abysmal." She looked past him, focusing on the pattern of the quilt beneath them. "It was a long time ago. I was in college."

"Abysmal, huh?" He dragged her up his body and playfully nuzzled her breasts.

"Totally," she murmured with a moan. "Just the opposite of this."

"I'm glad." He licked at her nipple, sending new streamers of fire directly into the center of her body.

"Me...too."

"Sh. Just let me love you now, Alexa, and let yourself feel everything."

"Why do you—?" she breathed, her gaze captured by the sensual promise just a heartbeat away.

"Because you're you," he interrupted. "Because you deserve the best, and because that's what you've given me."

He took an already tightly beaded nipple deep into his mouth while he trailed his fingers down her spine, smoothed them over the curve of her hips and then delved directly into the heat of her. He tormented, stroked and tantalized. He

again robbed her of her sanity. He brought her the treasures of the universe and made her understand that she was
his treasure. But, most of all, he filled his senses with the
memories that would eventually have to sustain him.

She writhed atop him, the tangled thickness of her hair
like a canopy of silk around them, her eyes closed as she al-
ternately panted and moaned. Bolts of lightning laced the
emotion she felt as Alexa willingly succumbed to the magic
that Gray brought to her throughout the night.

Alexa sighed quietly and shot a quick glance at Gray.
Seated beside her in the luxurious passenger section of the
Lear jet, his shoulders were rigid and his head was thrown
back against the top edge of his seat as he stared straight
ahead. He reminded her of a stone carving. She silently
mourned the tension between them, tension that felt so thick
it could have been sliced and buttered.

Daylight and reality, she concluded somewhat wistfully,
were a far cry from the romance of dancing under a circus
tent at a charity ball or a night spent testing the limits of
emotional and sensual control. She absently wondered if
she'd actually dreamed the entire night, but the subtle achi-
ness in her body assured her that she had not.

Fed up with the strain of enduring Alexa's persistent silence, Gray finally commented, "You're awfully quiet. I
don't think you've said two words since we left Dallas."

She smiled faintly, wondering just what he expected of
her. "You haven't said two words, either."

He frowned and shifted uneasily in his seat.

Alexa glanced out the oval window beside her. The blue
sky was filled with puffy little clouds that reminded her of
dabs of fluffy icing. The rolling hills of central California
stretched for as far as she could see below them.

"You're thinking about last night, aren't you?"

She looked back at him and nodded.

"Regrets?" he asked very tensely.

Her eyes widened. "None. What about you?"

"None," he replied, echoing her.

"I'm glad," she told him honestly. "I don't ever want to be remembered as someone who caused you regrets."

Gray, his body already rigid, flinched. He squeezed his hands into tight fists. Alexa noted the gesture, although she didn't understand its origin. She hated the fact that a night of utter joy would now be punctuated by his anger, but she was too confused and too tired to wonder just exactly what he was angry about.

They both lapsed into an awkward silence as the aircraft began its descent into Stockton. The pilot used the intercom to remind them to remain seated until they landed and the plane came to a complete stop.

"Alexa?"

"Yes?"

Searching for just the right words, he struggled to find a way to explain to her why he felt so uneasy.

Before he could speak, Alexa assured him, "You don't have to worry, you know. I'm not going to turn into some awful clinging vine just because we've made love. We're both adults, and we can keep what's happened in perspective. I didn't make love with you to try and trap you into anything, Gray."

"I know that," he answered harshly.

"Maybe I'm saying this the wrong way, but I don't want you to think you have to promise me anything because of what we've shared. I wanted to make love with you. Otherwise, I wouldn't have gone to Dallas."

The expression on her face proclaimed her sincerity. Gray knew she was trying to give him an out. Was he that obvious? And why did he feel so lousy all of a sudden?

His silence allowed her to continue. "I've got a lot of changes ahead of me. A relationship between us might end up complicating both our lives. So whatever happens between us at the ranch, happens. No strings attached. That way, no one gets hurt."

There, she thought. She'd made her little speech, the one she'd been rehearsing since getting aboard their flight. It left her feeling as hollow as she'd expected.

"That was quite a mouthful."

Stung by his biting tone, she said, "I'm just trying to let you know where I stand."

"Well, you're standing on very liberated ground, honey. In fact, you're the epitome of the modern woman. Happy now?"

No, she thought, *I'm not happy. I'm absolutely dying inside.* "I've simply said what needed saying," she defended stubbornly, capable of being equally mule-headed.

They deplaned, collected their luggage and returned to the ranch, silence reigning all the way. Michael, Will and Minna gathered to greet them as they pulled up in front of the house, smiling and eager to hear about the trip until, one by one, they noticed the tension between Alexa and Gray.

Although she tried to smile, all Alexa managed was a quiet, "It's good to be home," as she hugged everyone. Gray heard her comment and walked away, leaving them all slack-jawed at his abrupt behavior.

The next several days reminded Alexa of controlled chaos when she had a spare moment to even think about it. Carpenters converged on the ranch to construct a bandstand and outdoor buffet tables for the picnic. Delivery trucks bearing lamps and furniture, as well as crews of drapery installers, managed to show up every time things settled down to a dull roar.

The caterer and party consultant flitted about like escapees from an asylum for the deranged. For the most part, Alexa left them to their own devices. Any instructions she wanted conveyed to them she passed through Minna, who seemed up to coping with their bizarre personalities.

She ate her meals on the run. She frequently saw Gray, but neither seemed able to get beyond the basic amenities, which made Alexa feel like hired help. In spite of her feelings, she collapsed into bed each night, exhausted but proud of the fact that the preparations for both the cottages and the picnic were coming together on schedule.

Gray purposely left Alexa alone during their first few days back from Dallas. They both needed time to think, he told himself. But his conscience told him he was acting like a jerk.

He finally admitted to himself that he hadn't just opened his home to a stranger a little less than a month ago. He'd also opened his heart. But the past still edged his dreams for the future with fear, and he constantly fought the urge to simply tell Alexa how he felt about her and let the chips fall where they may.

She was so much like the wildflowers he'd taken her to see what felt like a lifetime ago. And like the wildflowers, she needed the freedom to grow and flourish on her own. She also seemed to need to be needed. He kept wondering if he'd misread the look in her eyes during the night they'd shared in Dallas. At the time, he'd thought it was love. Now, he wasn't so sure.

After enduring yet another sleepless night and going in repeated emotional circles, Gray gave into the sharp-edged desire tormenting him. He drew a sleeping Alexa from her bed in the guest room and carried her down the hall to the master suite just before dawn. He gently brought her out of a deep sleep with the teasing feel of his lips on her thighs and the soft caress of his fingertips stroking her nipples to pebble-hard points of arousal.

She arched into the sensations streaming into her body and sifting into her consciousness, discovering as she came awake that she was naked and no longer in her own bed. Her nightgown resembled a lemon silk snowdrift at the edge of the bed. He was stretched out nearby, his head near her hips and a seductive smile on his face as he stroked her willing body.

"I've been watching you sleep. You look like an angel."

She laughed, too happy to be with Gray to take him to task for spiriting her from her bed while she slept. "I look naked."

"A naked angel," he amended, willing to indulge her.

"How long have I been here?" she asked in a low, sexy, sleep-filled voice, flushing slightly when his lips and fingers grew bolder. She took a deep breath, then let it out suddenly as sparks raced along her nerve endings. She fell back against the pillows, desire pooling deep in her abdomen while the muscles in her body lost texture and substance.

"Not long. Maybe an hour or so. You sleep so deeply," he complained softly. His breath rushed, hot and deliciously arousing, across her silken thigh as he nibbled on the delicate flesh so close to her feminine core. "I didn't think you'd ever wake up."

Alexa trembled visibly and violently. She reached out, her hands finding an anchor as she grasped Gray's lowered head. "You're killing me," she whispered raggedly.

"I'll bring you back to life," he promised, his mouth avid, his fingers sinking into the curve of her hips as he brought her into even closer contact with his questing tongue and tender mouth.

"You should have wakened me," she scolded breathlessly. "I might've missed something important."

He lifted his head, his eyes dark with desire. Her comment made the edges of his sexy mouth twitch with laughter as he admitted, "The ranch has turned into Grand Central Station. You've always got a half dozen people following you around day and night. Besides, I wanted you to myself before the day started, and I didn't want you to say no. Desperate circumstances call for desperate deeds,'' he concluded, as though his actions were perfectly acceptable.

Her expression grew infinitely tender when she saw the fleeting hint of vulnerability in his eyes. "I don't think I could say no to you, Gray, not ever."

I love you nearly burst from her lips, but she managed to hold the words back by the sheer force of her will. She knew he didn't love her, but she had enough love for them both. That sense of emotional generosity made her want to give him everything she could, for as long as she could. Denying Gray anything would be like denying herself oxygen.

"Let me love you," he murmured as he closed his teeth ever so gently over her. He took her moan as her assent.

He guided her expertly through a maze of mind-shattering passion and nerve-disintegrating delight. Each time she gasped, he intensified his intimate stroking. Each time she whimpered, he delved deeper, held her more tightly. Each time she moaned his name, he savored his ability to give her pleasure. And when the heavens exploded, taking her consciousness and flinging it into the eternity of space, he knew that his life would be without meaning once she was gone.

Still quaking in the aftermath of a shattering climax, Alexa reached for Gray, her movements frenzied, her hands desperate as she tugged at him. He reluctantly, and only temporarily, relinquished his touch as he moved over her.

Her love gave her confidence, allowing her to take the initiative and share the responsibility he had assumed in Dallas. Sheathing him with the protection he kept nearby, her fingers shook as she touched him and then stroked him near to bursting. This simple act of intimacy forged another link between them and brought shudders to both of their bodies.

Looking down into her shining, passion-glazed eyes, his body suspended above her on trembling arms, Gray whispered, "I need you, Alexa. I need you so much."

Tears filled her eyes as he surged into her body in one swift thrust, tears of joy brought on by his admission that what he felt for her had finally surpassed wanting. Her last coherent thought was that while need wasn't love, it was the closest thing to it for a man governed by a fiercely independent nature and the painful lessons of loss he'd learned in the past.

Despite their efforts to delay the inevitable, release simultaneously detonated within them, startling them both with its intensity and threatening the barriers that separated them. Afterward, Alexa couldn't speak.

Held securely in Gray's arms, she quietly watched the sun shimmer over the land and filter into the master suite through the open balcony doors. Even as she watched, she listened to the beating of Gray's heart and tenderly swept her fingertips across his abdomen and down into the dense tangle of coarse hair that surrounded his sex.

Gray tensed and tightened his fingers on her hip as she sent him reeling with the simple touch of her fingertips. When he couldn't resist the streamers of flame running riot in his bloodstream any longer, he pulled her up so that they were nose to nose.

Alexa grinned at his fake frown and whispered, "Good morning."

He chuckled, amazed at her ability to rouse him to life so quickly. "Good morning, yourself. What do you think you're doing, Alexa?"

She gave him an innocent look, but her fingers didn't stop teasing. "Nothing much."

He captured her mouth in a hard kiss, lingering until she was gasping for air. "I'll show you nothing much," he promised when he gave her a chance to catch her breath.

He kept his promise, which accounted for their absence from breakfast that morning and their lack of sleep during the nights that followed.

The day before the picnic Alexa paused for a quick lunch in the kitchen. With everything on schedule, she felt safe stealing a few minutes for herself. The temporary cook house, set up on the far side of the back lawn, was a bee-hive of activity. Two chefs, several helpers and the caterer would spend the final hours before the arrival of the guests there. Because the staff was housed in one of the bunk-houses at the ranch and had permission to use the pool dur-ing their breaks, she felt certain that things would continue to run smoothly.

Alexa looked up from her sandwich and the checklist she'd been studying when the kitchen door slammed shut. Gray walked into the room, leaned down, gave her a body-weakening kiss and grinned as he pulled up a chair beside her.

She smiled at him, so content she practically slid off her chair. "You look pleased with yourself."

"Destiny just arrived."

"When can I see him?" she asked eagerly, motioning at him to help himself to a sandwich from the platter Minna had left for them.

Gray filled a plate and collected a napkin. "Later on to-night. He needs a little time to settle down. It's a long ride from Texas, in spite of an air-conditioned horse trailer that's outfitted with everything but a stereo system."

Alexa got up for a pitcher of lemonade that Minna al-ways kept cold. "From what I remember, he's absolutely spectacular, Gray. I hope he fulfills all your expectations."

His eyes gleamed as he watched her pour the tart drink into an ice-filled glass. Dressed casually in a cropped T-shirt, shorts and thongs, and with her hair gathered into a loose braid that trailed down the center of her back, she looked good enough to eat. "Speaking of expectations. Have I been fulfilling yours?"

She playfully smacked his hand when he tried to grope her breasts. "Watch your manners, Mr. Lennox. Anybody could walk in on us. And, yes, you've fulfilled *all* my expectations, and a few I didn't even know I had."

He tugged her down into his lap, his lunch momentarily forgotten. "Wanna play hooky?"

She hugged him, thinking just how much she'd miss simple moments like these. "I'd say yes in a minute if I thought I could spare the time. How about a late date tonight?"

"I don't know if I can hold out that long. I may have to tackle some hapless wench for temporary relief."

She arched a slender brow and tried to look menacing. "Try it and I'll break something critical for you. Some part of your anatomy that might come in handy later on tonight."

He saluted smartly and settled her back in her own chair. "Anything you say, ma'am."

She grinned and turned her attention to her lunch. Will and Minna wandered in from their chores and joined them a few minutes later.

Alexa wondered about Michael's absence during lunch, but she chalked it up to Destiny's arrival as she went in search of the florist who had set up shop in one of the empty barns.

Ten
___

Alexa burst into Gray's office late that afternoon, her face pale and her entire body shaking with worry. "Michael's gone. I can't find him anywhere. I thought it was strange when he didn't come in for lunch, but then I got involved with the florist and completely forgot about him. Every time I remembered that I hadn't seen him, some new problem with the picnic would crop up and I'd get sidetracked."

Startled by her hurried words and agitated behavior, Gray stood and quickly walked around his desk. "Calm down, Alexa. He's probably somewhere near Destiny's holding pen."

Her thick braid bounced as she shook her head. "No, he's not. I checked there first. Nobody's seen him all afternoon. I've looked everywhere, Gray. I've been looking for him for more than an hour now." Alexa's voice cracked. Tears filled her eyes. Dragging in a steadying breath, she grasped his arm as he towered over her. "I've searched and searched, and there's no sign of him. We've got to find him."

He brushed past her and strode toward his open office door. "Where's Will? Maybe he's seen Michael."

Will, already enlisted by Alexa to help search for Michael and just a few minutes behind her, stepped into view. "No, boss, I haven't seen him since this morning. I checked around after Miss Alexa told me she couldn't find him."

Gray turned to her. "Have Minna call the Wilcox boys. Find out if he played with them today."

Alexa didn't move. "I've already done that. Gray—"

"Stop talking and let me think," he ordered, anger edging his voice. Memories of the last four years crowded into his consciousness. Jenny, his sister, her husband. Their faces swam forward from the recesses of his mind. Panic momentarily threatened him with complete paralysis, but he shook it off. "It's almost time for supper. Why didn't you say anything sooner?"

Alexa paled even more. "I've already explained how busy I've been, and it seemed silly to tattle on him because he'd lost track of time. I really thought he'd wander in at any minute. You know how he's always popping up wherever I am. Then I had to sort out a problem with the waiters and—"

"No more excuses, Alexa," he broke in tersely before turning back to Will. "Have you checked the saddle horses?"

The older man nodded. "Bayou wandered in ten minutes ago . . . still saddled."

A muscle jumped in Gray's jaw, emphasizing his grim expression. "I gave Michael permission to use him if he wanted to go riding." He swore, the words harsh and explicit. "Get everyone up to the main house and coordinate a search party. Use the grid map on the wall in the library. One walkie-talkie to each search group. I'll take the Jeep and check the north edge of the ranch. It's too dangerous up there for a man on horseback after sundown. Have Minna notify the neighbors and ask them to drive out along our adjoining property lines. Double-check all the barns, storage sheds, holding pens and pastures before you send anyone out.''

"Right away, boss."

"What can I do to help?" Alexa asked.

"Just stay out of the way. That'll be a start."

Stricken by his tone, she stared at him. Gray studied her with hard eyes and a hostile expression. She shifted nervously but didn't break eye contact. "He's been so happy, especially since he's been working around the horses. I never expected him to run away," she finished, worry nearly choking her.

Gray clenched his fists as he spoke. "I'll never forgive either one of us if anything happens to him, Alexa. *Never*." His jaw tightly clenched, he walked to his desk and reached for his hat, keys and a pair of leather gloves.

"I'm going with you," she announced, regaining a measure of her natural spirit. "You might need me. I'll be ready to go in five minutes."

"I don't need any more interference," he barked, but he knew she was right, just as he knew that they were both poised on the razor-sharp edge of a potential tragedy if Michael didn't turn up soon.

"You've got it whether or not you want it." She turned on her heel and left his office. Alexa hurried to the house and changed into sturdier clothes and shoes. She was waiting for Gray when he slid behind the wheel of the Jeep.

"I've brought a thermos of hot coffee, some fruit and two flashlights."

He shot her a quelling look then ignored her as he pulled away from the house. Too worried about Michael to deal with his anger, she scanned the surrounding countryside as they drove up and down a teeth-jarring network of back roads that covered the ranch's extensive acreage.

She knew he blamed her. Since she already blamed herself for Michael's disappearance, Alexa didn't begrudge Gray his hostile feelings. She ransacked her mind for a hint or a clue that the boy might have given them as they searched for him. She found nothing. Darkness converged on the land, but they continued, the headlights and a searchlight fixed to the front hood of the Jeep the only illumination they could depend on as the moon drifted behind a bank of clouds.

Rain intermittently spattered the windshield as night wore on. The dirt roads disappeared as routinely as they reappeared, forcing Gray to navigate the uneven terrain at a cautious pace. Glancing at him, Alexa saw his strain in the rigid set of his shoulders and his tightly clenched jaw.

"We have to go back," he said a short while later.

Alexa looked at the gas gauge, understood why and kept quiet.

Gray felt numb as he drove back to the main house. He parked at the gas pump after sounding the horn to alert Will to his presence. Operating on automatic as he filled the gas tank, he couldn't get the image of his sister and brother-in-law, or the accident that had taken them, out of his mind. They'd died quickly, but he still recalled every horrifying second and every agonizing sound of that night.

Michael had been knocked unconscious just seconds after the drunk driver had plowed into them. Gray remembered being trapped in the car, the pungent odor of leaking fuel nearly suffocating him, and his sense of utter helplessness as he'd waited to be pried out of the twisted wreckage. He'd nearly died that night, then he'd spent the next three months in the hospital praying for death so that he wouldn't have to relive the nightmare.

Alexa didn't get out of the Jeep while Gray talked to Will. He slid into the driver's seat and they set out again. She poured coffee when he asked; she handed him an apple a little while later, even though he hadn't requested it. He ate automatically, every sense alert to even the subtlest change in the terrain he knew as well as the creases and calluses of his own hands.

He pulled to a stop sometime near midnight, exhausted, discouraged and still silent. When he leaned forward and rested his head against the steering wheel, she offered quiet comfort by rubbing his shoulders. Gray finally looked up and peered into the darkness again. A few seconds later, he froze. Alexa instantly felt the change in him.

"What is it?" she asked, hopeful for the first time all night as she peered into the same darkness that seemed to fascinate Gray.

He didn't answer, but switched off the headlights and searchlight instead. Up ahead, if his tired eyes weren't playing tricks on him, was a flicker of light. He flipped the headlights back on and put the Jeep into gear, edging slowly across the rutted ground.

Alexa exhaled softly and dug her fingers into the leather seat. Tension billowed off Gray, unrelenting waves of stress that she felt and longed to soothe away. "Can't we go any faster?" she finally asked.

Gray shook his head. "The land up here's unstable. It's a maze of underground tunnels and shallow caves. Several have already collapsed."

Alarmed, Alexa moved forward to the edge of her seat and watched the flow of uneven ground. "Does Michael know the danger?"

He paused, considering her question. "He may remember."

"Why would he come out here in the first place?"

"There's a small lake about a mile east of here. His mother used to take him there for picnics when they visited."

Gray stopped the Jeep and turned off the engine. He left the lights on. A small figure sat huddled by a camp fire about fifty yards in front of them. "I'll go the rest of the way on foot."

Alexa slid out of her seat after fishing the flashlights from the bag that held the thermos. She met Gray at the front of the Jeep and handed him one. "I'm right behind you."

"You're damned persistent," he noted roughly.

She ignored his ire. "Let's go get Michael."

A few moments later they heard a tremulous voice call out, "Uncle Gray?" The voice, attached to the small body now poised beside the camp fire, was clear, curious and painfully familiar.

"We're here, Michael. Stay put and we'll be right with you," Gray told him while he could still speak.

Alexa breathed, "Thank God."

Uncle Gray. The words echoed in his head as they made their way to the camp site. Michael hadn't addressed him as Uncle Gray since before the accident.

"I knew you'd find me," he said, his pleasure evident. "I remembered everything you taught me, Uncle Gray. After Bayou got spooked by a rabbit and ran off, I gathered up some firewood and stones and made a camp fire. I was real careful so I wouldn't start a brush fire or nothing bad like that. And I stayed put so I wouldn't get lost and you could find me. I even remembered to bring my canteen, just like you told me I should if I ever went off exploring. Did you know there's all kinds of caves and stuff up here? Why don't we have a real camp out sometime and dig for gold? I bet there's still some around here."

Gray felt emotion rise up inside him like an advancing tide. It clogged his throat and brought tears to his eyes. He dropped to his knees beside his nephew and gathered him into his arms, suddenly very aware of just how much he loved this vulnerable child. Michael might have his mother's eyes and his father's adventuresome nature, but he was special simply because he was Michael Lennox Hamilton. Gray instantly resolved that the past would remain in the past. He would never permit it to harm his relationship with the boy again.

Alexa brushed at the tears of relief streaming down her cheeks and carefully made her way back to the Jeep. Gray and Michael needed the privacy of the moment. She contacted Will with the walkie-talkie while the two lingered at the campfire.

As she poured herself a cup of coffee, she decided that this night might be the turning point in what was fast becoming a nearly mended relationship, as well as the end of another. Sipping the tepid liquid, Alexa waited for nearly an hour while the two talked.

Michael fell asleep in her lap during the drive back to the ranch. Gray carried him upstairs to his room while Alexa waited for Gray in his library.

He walked into the room a short time later, paused at the bar and splashed cognac into a snifter. Emotionally and physically drained, he sank onto the leather couch beside Alexa and leaned his head back against the cushions.

"I apologize, Gray. What happened to Michael could have been avoided if I'd been paying closer attention to him." She thought of the dangerous tunnels and unstable earth where they'd found him and trembled.

When he didn't say anything, she glanced at him and found him staring at her, an expression of stark shock on his face. "What in hell are you talking about?"

She cleared her throat and got herself under control. "It's really very simple. I let the picnic get in the way of my common sense. I also forgot that he's just a little boy who probably felt lost in the shuffle. I hope you'll both be able to forgive me some day.''

"Alexa, we all make mistakes. We just do the best we can with what we've got. Any more than that's impossible. And for the record, none of what happened tonight was your fault, and that includes my lousy temper. Michael knows he shouldn't have gone off without telling someone. *He* made the mistake, so there's damn well nothing to forgive. All I care about right now is that the boy's safe and upstairs in his own bed." He glanced at his watch, the subject of right and wrong forgotten, and grimaced. "Do you realize how late it is?"

"Unfortunately, I do." She still wasn't finished berating herself over the situation with Michael, but she was too exhausted to continue until she'd gotten some sleep.

They wearily climbed the stairs together. Alexa trudged down the hall to the guest room after saying good night. Gray, too tired to question her odd mood, entered the master suite.

She stripped down to the skin, not bothering with a gown, and crawled into bed, her thoughts on the reality that had haunted her since finding Michael. In less than three days she would no longer have a reason to remain at the ranch.

Gray strode into her room soon after, mumbling something about Mohammed and mountains as he got into bed beside her and gathered her into his arms. Despite the stress of the last eight hours, despite their fatigue and despite the hard words they'd exchanged earlier in the evening, neither one could sleep. The instant Gray smoothed his fingertips across her breasts and down her flat stomach, Alexa surged against him.

What began as a tender foray into the gentler boundaries of passion soon began to resemble the detonating impact of exploding dynamite. While Gray started out as seducer, Alexa almost immediately became the aggressor. She couldn't keep her hands or her mouth still, nor did she try. Amazed by the almost desperate wildness of her actions, Gray let her have her way, following her lead as she orchestrated, in an almost frenzied manner, the intense sensations exploding between them.

At one point in the sensual melee that followed, Alexa vaguely realized that she was losing all control. Focused on Gray, who had become the center of her consciousness, and on the muscled texture and furnacelike heat of his body, she didn't care. Time between them would soon be reduced to a few days, then a few hours, and then even fewer minutes. Two hundred people would populate Lennox Ranch by midmorning. Privacy would be impossible. This night might be their last real night of intimacy.

Kneeling between his spread legs, she leaned forward and began to captivate him by slowly running the tips of her fingernails from his broad shoulders, across his muscled chest, down through the thick pelt of dark hair that covered his belly and finally, with shattering deftness, into the nest of coarser hair that framed his jutting desire. She touched him there and he moaned, the sound raw, earthy and gloriously male. She trembled, then released an achingly soft sigh that reached inside him like a gentle caress.

"Alexa, come here. I can't take any more of this."

"Not yet," she whispered, still intent on weaving her spell. She knew she couldn't quit until she'd pushed him to the very edge of his control. Only then would she give in to him. Only then would she know him as intimately as she needed to know him before she left. The memories they made tonight would have to hold her for a long time, maybe even forever.

They watched one another. Her gaze scorched him and her fingertips tortured, but it was a pleasure-filled kind of torture he embraced with body and soul. He gritted his teeth and his dark eyes blazed like unbanked fires as he stared at her. She sent him tumbling into a continuous sensory free-fall as she seductively stroked and teased.

"Now you're killing *me*," he whispered raggedly.

"Then I'll bring you back to life," she promised, just as he had so recently.

And she did, but slowly, almost painfully, taking him to the edge, bringing him back, testing his control and taunting his senses until he cried out again and again. She gloried in the feeling of feminine power that raged inside her.

Gray reached the limit of his restraint, teetered on the brink for the longest time and then wrenched free of Alexa. he dragged her up his long, lean body, holding her above him so that he could suckle her breasts. He felt them swell and firm as her nipples simultaneously transformed into aroused nuggets as his tongue returned the torture she had just bestowed on him. He was ruthless, loving and marvelously seductive, and he had her writhing like a wild thing in a matter of seconds.

He moved her so that she sat astride him, but he didn't take the final step. Instead, he kept teething and suckling, driving her insane with his mouth and tongue. She clutched his shoulders, uttered broken little cries that spurred him on before she shifted her hips in an urgent physical plea. She struggled to bring them into intimate contact but couldn't quite accomplish the connection she craved.

Gray heard her shattered moan of frustration. Far too aroused to ignore it and far too desperate for more of her, he moved just enough to give her what she wanted. She jerked against him, hungry for penetration as she took him into her body and into her heart.

They spiraled upward, rocketing toward release. Gray fiercely clasped her to his heart and he surged into her. Tears streamed down Alexa's cheeks as she repeatedly whispered his name. She was still whispering his name when they exploded together.

She lay sprawled across his chest in the aftermath of their lovemaking, too replete to even consider moving. She fell asleep that way, her hands still twined around his neck and their bodies still intimately joined.

Gray held her for several hours, savoring the utter comfort and peace of having her in his arms while he pretended that their relationship could go on forever. Shortly after dawn, he returned to the master suite to get ready for the first day of the picnic.

Any questions Alexa might have asked about waking up alone remained unvoiced. She awoke to the sound of laughter, soft Spanish-style guitar music and animated conversations drifting up through the open balcony doors from the pool area. The clock told her it was nearly noon, which accounted for her rested condition. It also told her that she was very late.

After showering and dressing, she hurried downstairs and stepped outside to greet several of the people she'd met in Dallas. Their easy acceptance of her role as Gray's hostess instantly relaxed her.

The men spent most of their time talking horses, while several of the women, having brought their children along at Gray's invitation, gathered in poolside groups and supervised the water sports. Others eagerly toured the thoroughbred facility, lingered at the oval racetrack to watch the yearlings learn racing etiquette, enviously admired the stallions that stood at stud at the ranch, or indulged in one of several activities planned for them by their host.

Alexa and Gray caught frequent glances of one another as the first day of the picnic unfolded. But the presence of nearly two hundred guests, the press people sent to chronicle the gathering of the horse-racing world's elite, and the constant demands on Alexa's time by the caterer, kept their contact brief and conversation reduced to a minimum.

It was late when the buses began transporting people back to the Stockton hotel, so late that Alexa didn't question Gray's absence from her bed that night. After being on the go all day, she gratefully slipped under the covers and slept a solid eight hours before she resumed her hostessing duties.

Alexa supervised Sunday morning brunch, which was set up on the sprawling, manicured lawn in front of the elegant three-story white Victorian farmhouse. Candy-striped pink and white tents provided shade from the sun as the guests sampled the extensive array of food prepared for them.

As she stood on the veranda and surveyed the crowd, she noticed a long black limo coming up the gravel drive. Alexa automatically assumed it carried a late-arriving guest. When her father emerged from the vehicle, she could only stare.

Gray, chatting with several men at the far end of the buffet line, glanced up in time to see the shocked look on her face. He managed to extricate himself from the small group and began to navigate through the crowd, but each person he passed seemed intent on speaking with him. Stuck in the middle of the throng, he saw Alexa greet a tall, distinguished-looking, silver-haired man who appeared to be in his fifties, and escort him into the house.

Once inside the privacy of Gray's library, Alexa slowly turned to face Jack Rivers. "I'm surprised to see you, Father."

"I thought it was about time we talked." He walked around the room, nodding appreciatively when he noticed two Leroy Neiman originals on the wall.

"You're right," she said, struggling for composure, "but it might be best if we wait until I get home."

Jack stopped his aimless strolling and took a seat in one of two leather wing chairs positioned in front of the fireplace. "You've been gone a month now, Alexa. It's time for you to stop running away from your life."

She stiffened at his authoritative tone. "It's up to me to decide what I will and won't do, Father."

He exhaled quietly, the lines around his mouth and his eyes deepening as he regarded her. She suddenly saw his age, something she'd never really noticed before. Off balance, she asked the first question that popped into her head. "Does Tom still have a future with Rivers International?"

"Why wouldn't he?"

"You tell me," she challenged, standing her ground.

"Tom Henderson will be the next president of R.I. I don't mix business decisions with personal disappointments. Surely you know that much about me, Alexa."

She nodded, hesitated for a moment, then admitted, "I know about you and Mother. I found her diaries the morning of the wedding." She saw surprise flicker briefly in his faded blue eyes. "And I know I'm not your real daughter."

"I'm sorry you found out," he told her, genuine regret in his expression. "I'd hoped you never would."

"I'm glad I know. It helps me understand why you never liked me and never really wanted to be my father."

"Alexa! You're my daughter. I don't dislike you. I..." He hesitated awkwardly. "I care a great deal about you."

"Is that why you've always ignored me?" she burst out. "Is that why you never let me talk about Mother after she died? Is that why you sent me away to school and wouldn't let me come home for holidays? Is that why I spent my childhood feeling like a piece of excess baggage?" She was shaking and pale by the time she finished.

Jack frowned. "Come and sit down before you fall down."

Alexa did sit down, but because *she* decided that it was her best course of action at the moment. Her knees felt like limp rubber bands as she eased into the chair adjacent to his. "Talk to me, Father. Tell me why I was the one who paid the price for what was wrong between you and Mother. I really want to understand. I've tried so hard to put myself in your place, and I've tried to understand how betrayed and disappointed you must have felt when you learned the truth, but shutting me out of your life was wrong."

"What do you really want from me, Alexa?"

"A *real* relationship. Friendship, at the very least. Mutual respect. Maybe even your love, but I can wait for that since it's not the kind of thing a person can just order up like fast food. And no more performance pressure, no matter how subtle," she concluded.

Several minutes passed before he spoke. "I'm not an emotional man, Alexa. I do well with facts and figures, but I've never quite known how to deal with you. And you're right, I *was* deeply hurt by your mother's lies, but what hurt more was not having a son or daughter of my own." He got up and paced for a few moments. Alexa watched him, suddenly realizing that this was as difficult for him as it was for her. He finally turned and looked at her. "I loved your mother, Alexa. She's the only woman I've ever loved."

Shocked, she said, "But all you both ever did was fight!"

"We had our good moments, too, but we were two stubborn people trapped in an impossible marriage, a marriage we should have ended long before your mother died. She was indulged and spoiled by her parents, and I didn't want you growing up that way. I just wanted you strong and independent so that you could take over the company one day."

"I don't want Rivers International. I never did. All I've ever wanted was to be a teacher."

He nodded. "Considering your obsession with Rivers House, I don't suppose that should surprise me." They were both quiet for a moment. "I know we can't change the past, but I'd be willing to try this friendship idea of yours."

She stood and walked toward him. "On one condition."

He arched a silver brow. The look on his face didn't dissuade her from speaking. "I've spent most of my life trying to please you, but that's pretty much a thing of the past now. I hope you can find a way to accept me for who I am and respect my right to make my own choices. I'll ask for advice when I need it, but whatever happens, whether I succeed or fail, I want your promise that you won't judge me."

He smiled down at her. "You've turned into quite a little tyrant, haven't you?"

"I guess I'm my father's daughter, after all," she said archly, making her way to the library doors and pulling them open.

He scowled at that, but the teasing expression on her face kept him from being annoyed with her. Jack Rivers followed his daughter to the library doors, grudging respect in his eyes as he watched her. Before they stepped into the hallway, he asked, "When are you coming home, Alexa?"

"The day after tomorrow. I've already booked a flight."

Gray, striding down the hallway toward the library, clearly heard both the deep-voiced question and Alexa's reply. His footsteps faltered. His heart went a little crazy in his chest.

"I want you to meet Grayson Lennox," Alexa said, unaware that he stood only a few feet away.

"I know who the man is, Alexa. At least credit me with thoroughness. I also know about your car and your injury, which appears to have healed nicely."

She smiled, knowing that her father would never change but loving him anyway. "Then you know I totaled the car."

He nodded. "There's no need to take a commercial flight. I'll wait for you while you pack. We can go home together. I've got the corporate jet waiting for me in Stockton."

She stumbled mentally as she searched for a reply to his offer, which, on the surface, was hardly out of line. "I don't think—"

Gray stepped into view and spoke up. "I don't believe I've met your guest, Alexa." Inside his mind, another voice cried, *You can't leave yet! I won't let you leave. I need you here.*

When she didn't speak, just stared at Gray, Jack Rivers stepped forward and introduced himself. Alexa finally found her voice. "I need to go upstairs for a few minutes. Why don't you two get acquainted? Maybe you'd like to stay for brunch if you have the time, Father." She didn't wait for his answer.

Both men watched her climb the stairs. From Jack's expression it was clear to Gray that he was puzzled by her odd behavior. As for himself, Gray wanted to grab her and shake some sense into her. What did she mean by saying she was leaving?

One powerful man faced another. Eye to eye, each openly measured the other. After a few tense moments and silent acknowledgement of their equality, despite the differences in their ages and respective worlds, Gray escorted Alexa's father out to the buffet line, certain he wouldn't lack for company as the older man greeted several friends. He then made a beeline back to the house, taking three steps at a time when he charged up the staircase.

Gray paused in the doorway of the guest room, confused when he didn't immediately see Alexa. A flash of dark teal, the color of her long cotton gauze hostess gown, revealed that she was standing at the balcony railing. He moved across the room, his gaze riveted on her. She stood very still, her head bowed and her hands pressed to her cheeks.

"Marry me, Alexa."

She flinched under the harshness of his commanding tone. She slowly turned around. Uncertainty flooded her as she looked up at him and frantically searched his face. Any hope she momentarily felt died a painful death when she noted the lack of emotion in his expression.

"Marry me, Alexa," he demanded again. "We like each other, and we're good friends. We have a lot in common, and you're the only woman I know who doesn't cringe every time I raise my voice or lose my temper. I know you love the ranch. I'm a wealthy man, so I can afford to give you almost anything you'd ever want. We'd be good parents to Michael if anything happens to his grandparents. And we both want children. You understand me, Alexa...and you love what I do to you in bed," he finished, thinking he'd just given her every reason in the world to remain at the ranch. Guilt assaulted him almost instantly, because he hadn't said a single word about how much he loved her.

Anger dented, then penetrated her shock. "Have you completely lost your mind?" she snapped, livid that he was turning what should have been a question asked with love and tenderness into some kind of heartless merger proposal.

"No, damn it, I haven't lost my mind. You're the one who's been running around here searching out responsibility like it's some kind of a cure for the common cold. Well, it worked. You've made yourself necessary. I need you. Since you need to be needed, we've obviously got a match."

"We don't have anything of the kind." She marched toward the balcony doors, glaring up at him when he stepped into her path and grabbed her by the shoulders as she tried to brush by him.

"I want you, Alexa."

"Tough! I don't want you, especially not with some cold-blooded marriage contract hanging over my head for the rest of my life."

He tried another tack. "I need you. I have since the night you wrapped your fancy little imported sports car around my corner oak."

"Then hire somebody to take my place. Heavens! Run an ad in the Stockton paper. Wanted—one needy, outspoken female with nerves of steel who's also a reckless driver. Or should it read a needy outspoken female with a tongue that could *penetrate* steel, with the temper of a shrew who crashes cars specifically into oak trees? I forget right now, but I'm sure you'll remember when it comes time to call the paper." She jerked out from under his heavy hands, shoved at him and then dashed into the guest room.

He strode into the room, not two steps behind her. "What in the world's wrong with you today?"

She ignored him and headed for the closet. Tugging out one of her suitcases, she dumped it, unzipped, on the seaman's chest at the end of her bed. Ignoring Gray, she yanked open a bureau drawer, gathered up the contents, turned around and flung a collection of nightgowns into the yawning piece of luggage. All the while, she prayed that she wouldn't start crying before she got away from him.

He came after her and seized her before she could scoop another load of clothes out of another drawer. "Alexa, stop this and talk to me. What's wrong?"

Her blue-gray eyes blazed fire as she wrenched free of him for the second time in as many minutes. Looking up at him, seeing his confusion and the vulnerability in his eyes, she finally relented.

Very quietly and very deliberately, Alexa told him the truth. "*You're* what's wrong with me, Gray. I'm in love with you. I want to spend my entire life loving you. I want to go to bed with you every night, and I want to wake up next to you every morning. I want to have your babies. I want to rub your back when you're tense and out of sorts. I want to overdose on your sensuality. I even want to fight with you and then make up. In short, I want to have a life with you, but I can't.''

He looked incredulous. "Why not?"

"Because you're too afraid that you'll lose me if you tell me that you love me," she announced, the starkness of the truth wounding them both in different ways. "I grew up in a loveless home, Gray, but I'm not afraid to love. You grew up surrounded by love, but you're terrified of the risks you associate with loving. You're the strongest, toughest man I've ever met, yet love frightens you. I think that's very sad, because your fear is about to rob us of a future together. I watched fear and pride destroy my parents, and I won't ever willingly set myself up for that kind of heartache, no matter how much I love you.''

Too stunned by her admission of love and her insightful description of the man he'd become to disagree with her, Gray crossed the room and stepped out onto the balcony. Concerned over him because of his silence and the stricken look on his face, Alexa followed him. She stood beside him as he stared out across his land, praying that he might find a way to overcome his fear.

While Gray struggled with the emotions coursing through him, Alexa began to speak again, but so softly that he had to strain to hear the words. "I never really felt the confidence I always wanted to feel about myself as a woman until I came here. I've discovered all kinds of things about myself, some good and some bad. Loving you has freed me, Gray. It's also helped me understand that whatever else I do, I can't agree to accept only the part of you that you feel safe revealing.''

She looked up at him, her eyes filled with tears, her love reflected in her brimming eyes. "Loving is trusting your partner. I want the whole man, and if you can't trust me in the same way that I'm willing to trust you, then how can we possibly have a life together?''

Resistance and fear, the twin coils that had bound hi
heart for nearly four years, began to unravel within Gray
He slipped his arm around Alexa and drew her against him
He felt intense shame that he couldn't admit his feeling
while Alexa willingly abandoned all the self-protective in
stincts that she'd used as a shield during her first weeks a
the ranch.

She exhibited courage and strength, two characteristic
he'd long credited himself with, but now he knew he'd bee
wrong. He wasn't either, not if he let this woman walk away
from him simply because he feared the truth of his ow
emotions.

On the verge of giving up hope, Alexa felt him trembl
and instinctively tightened the supportive arm she'd slippe
around his waist. His vulnerability gave her the will to shar
her thoughts one last time.

"I want your love, Gray, if that's what you feel for me
but I need to hear the words. I want all the joy and emo
tional security attached to being loved by you. Your silenc
would eventually drive us apart, because simply knowin
you love me won't be enough. I want the words, Gray. I de
serve them, and I can't and won't settle for anything less."

Alexa fell silent, waiting for him to speak and praying tha
he would be able to break out of the emotional prison he'
lived in for the last few years.

Something shattered inside him, some final barrier h
suddenly realized he no longer needed if it meant Alex
would share a life with him. He embraced her, bringing he
up on her toes as he lowered his head and kissed her, an al
consuming, completely combustible kiss that sent her nerv
endings into frenzied shock. His tongue ravished as h
mouth crushed.

She reveled in it, giving back in full everything she re
ceived from him. Gray had broken through his fear. Alex

could feel it in the possessiveness of his arms and in the unrestrained passion coming directly from his heart.

He finally lifted his head and smiled down at her, the look on his face one of blinding revelation. He laughed joyfully as he hugged her. "I love you. Dear God, I love you more than I thought I'd love anyone ever again."

"Again, say it again," she whispered, clinging to him as he lifted her into his arms and carried her the length of the balcony to the open doors of the master suite.

"I love you, Alexa." He whipped her clothes from her so quickly that she couldn't have protested even if she'd wanted to. His disappeared with the speed of light. She laughed, enthralled with his spontaneous behavior.

"I love you, too. Oh, Gray, I love you so much." She flung her arms around him, knocked him backward and sent him sprawling across the bed with her exuberance. She landed on top of him.

"I think we should talk to your father. And we should definitely get married."

"Later. Much later," Alexa whispered, intent on tantalizing him with her busy fingers and nibbling lips and teasing tongue even as he plied her body with equal commitment and intensity.

"Later," Gray agreed, groaning as she sent a fireball of emotion and sensation spinning into the center of his heart.

His focus shifted completely to the woman in his arms, the woman who cared enough to understand him, the woman who loved him without reservation, the same woman who would stand up to him as stubbornly as she would stand at his side for the rest of their lives.

* * * * *

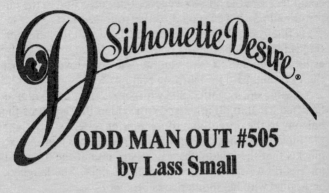

"GIVE YOUR HEART TO SILHOUETTE" SWEEPSTAKES
OFFICIAL RULES
NO PURCHASE NECESSARY TO ENTER OR RECEIVE A PRIZE

1. To enter and join the Silhouette Reader Service, rub off the concealment device on all game tickets. This will reveal the potential value for each Sweepstakes entry number and the number of free book(s) you will receive. Accepting the free book(s) will automatically entitle you to also receive a free bonus gift. If you do not wish to take advantage of our introduction to the Silhouette Reader Service but wish to enter the Sweepstakes only, rub off the concealment device on tickets #1-3 only. To enter, return your entire sheet of tickets. Incomplete and/or inaccurate entries are not eligible for that section or section (s) of prizes. Not responsible for mutilated or unreadable entries or inadvertent printing errors. Mechanically reproduced entries are null and void.

2. Either way, your Sweepstakes numbers will be compared against the list of winning numbers generated at random by computer. In the event that all prizes are not claimed, random drawings will be made from all entries received from all presentations to award all unclaimed prizes. All cash prizes are payable in U.S. funds. This is in addition to any free, surprise or mystery gifts that might be offered. The following prizes are awarded in this sweepstakes:

(1)	*Grand Prize	$1,000,000 Annuity
(1)	First Prize	$35,000
(1)	Second Prize	$10,000
(3)	Third Prize	$5,000
(10)	Fourth Prize	$1,000
(25)	Fifth Prize	$500
(5000)	Sixth Prize	$5

*The Grand Prize is payable through a $1,000,000 annuity. Winner may elect to receive $25,000 a year for 40 years, totaling up to $1,000,000 without interest, or $350,000 in one cash payment. Winners selected will receive the prizes offered in the Sweepstakes promotion they receive.

Entrants may cancel the Reader Service privileges at any time without cost or obligation to buy (see details in center insert card).

Versions of this Sweepstakes with different graphics may be offered in other mailings or at retail outlets by Torstar Corp. and its affiliates. This promotion is being conducted under the supervision of Marden-Kane, Inc., an independent judging organization. By entering this Sweepstakes, each entrant accepts and agrees to be bound by these rules and the decisions of the judges, which shall be final and binding. Odds of winning are dependent upon the total number of entries received. Taxes, if any, are the sole responsibility of the winners. Prizes are nontransferable. All entries must be received by March 31, 1990. The drawing will take place on April 30, 1990, at the offices of Marden-Kane, Inc., Lake Success, N.Y.

This offer is open to residents of the U.S., Great Britain and Canada, 18 years or older, except employees of Torstar Corp., its affiliates, and subsidiaries, Marden-Kane, Inc. and all other agencies and persons connected with conducting this Sweepstakes. All federal, state and local laws apply. Void wherever prohibited or restricted by law.

Winners will be notified by mail and may be required to execute an affidavit of eligibility and release that must be returned within 14 days after notification. Canadian winners will be required to answer a skill-testing question. Winners consent to the use of their name, photograph and/or likeness for advertising and publicity in conjunction with this and similar promotions without additional compensation. One prize per family or household.

For a list of our most current major prizewinners, send a stamped, self-addressed envelope to: WINNERS LIST, c/o MARDEN-KANE, INC., P.O. BOX 701, SAYREVILLE, N.J. 08871

Sweepstakes entry form is missing, please print your name and address on a 3" x 5" piece of plain paper and send to:

In the U.S.	In Canada
Sweepstakes Entry	Sweepstakes Entry
901 Fuhrmann Blvd.	P.O. Box 609
P.O. Box 1867	Fort Erie, Ontario
Buffalo, NY 14269-1867	L2A 5X3

LTY-S69R

Silhouette Desire ®

COMING NEXT MONTH

#505 ODD MAN OUT—Lass Small
July's *Man of the Month*, Graham Rawlins, was undeniably attractive, but Roberta Lambert seemed uninterested. However, Graham was very determined, and she found he'd do almost *anything* to get her attention....

#506 THE PIRATE O'KEEFE—Helen R. Myers
Doctor Laura Connell was intrigued by the injured man washed up on her beach. When she discovered his true identity it was too late—she'd fallen for the pirate O'Keefe.

#507 A WILDER NAME—Laura Leone
Luke Swain was positively the most irritating man Nina Gnagnarelli had ever met. He'd insulted her wardrobe, her integrity and her manners. He'd also set her heart on fire!

#508 BLIND JUSTICE—Cathryn Clare
As far as Lily Martineau was concerned, successful corporate lawyer Matt Malone was already married—to his job. Matt pleaded guilty as charged, then demanded a retrial.

#509 ETERNALLY EVE—Ashley Summers
Nate Wright had left Eve Sheridan with a broken heart. Now he seemed to have no memory of her—but it was a night Eve would never forget!

#510 MAGIC TOUCH—Noelle Berry McCue
One magic night with a handsome stranger made Caroline Barclay feel irresistible. But she didn't believe in fairy tales until James Mitchel walked back into her life—as her new boss.

AVAILABLE NOW:

#499 IRRESISTIBLE
Annette Broadrick

#500 EYE OF THE STORM
Sara Chance

#501 WILDFLOWER
Laura Taylor

#502 THE LOVING SEASON
Cait London

#503 MOON SHADOW
Janice Kaiser

#504 SHARING CALIFORNIA
Jeanne Stephens

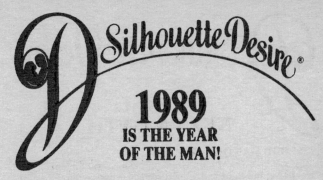

Silhouette Desire ®

1989
IS THE YEAR
OF THE MAN!

What makes a romance? A special man, of course, and Silhouette Desire cele-
brates that fact with *twelve* of them! From Mr. January to Mr. December, every
month has a tribute to the Silhouette Desire hero—our **MAN OF THE MONTH!**

Sexy, macho, charming, irritating . . . irresistible! Nothing can stop these men
from sweeping you away. Created by some of your favorite authors, each man is
custom-made for pleasure—*reading* pleasure—so don't miss a single one.

Mr. July is Graham Rawlins in ODD MAN OUT by Lass Small
Mr. August is Jeremy Kincaid in MOUNTAIN MAN by Joyce Thies
Mr. September is Clement Cornelius Barto in BEGINNER'S LUCK by Dixie
Browning
Mr. October is James Branigan in BRANIGAN'S TOUCH by Leslie Davis
Guccione
Mr. November is Shiloh Butler in SHILOH'S PROMISE by BJ James
Mr. December is Tad Jackson in WILDERNESS CHILD by Ann Major

So get out there and find your man!

Silhouette Desire's

MAN OF THE MONTH . . .

MOM-1R